TARA'S TRIALS

ROMANCE ON THE OREGON TRAIL BOOK 4

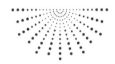

KATHLEEN BALL

I dedicate this book to the fans that stuck with me while I did this series!
As always I dedicate this book to Bruce, Steven, Colt, Clara and Mavis because I love them.

CHAPTER ONE

*A*fter walking for what seemed forever, Tara Carmichael stumbled into Fort Bridger, her heart sinking in dismay at the ramshackle place. "Please," she asked a young boy brushing down a mule outside a rickety barn. "I need to speak with whoever's in charge." Her gaze darted about, seeking any sign of people. "Are there any soldiers here?"

Eyes wide, the boy shook his head. "Mr. Sutter at the store's in charge o' things."

Clutching the torn bodice on her dress together, Tara stumbled into the store at, which was just as empty of people as the fort. Shelves and counters held all manner of cooking staples, flour, ground corn, small bags of sugar. To her left, hunting and trapping supplies. To her right, a counter was heaped with yard goods, serviceable fabric in practical colors. A few plaid men's shirts were neatly folded and stacked to one side. On a line strung across the small space hung a few cotton dresses already made up.

A bent and wrinkled little man approached, a tired but friendly enough smile on his face. "Can I help you, ma'am?"

His sharp eyes raked her slight form, no doubt taking in the tattered state of her clothing, the dirt smudging her face.

She opened her mouth to ask about soldiers, but something in his stare made her aware she was not covered well. "I... I need some clothes," she said, unable to keep the quiet desperation from seeping into her voice.

"Got some dresses made up there," he pointed to the line of clothes that she would have had to be blind to not see.

She cast a wistful eye to the fancy fabrics and colors. "I don't... have little money..." *Or any money, actually...*

His smile dimmed. "Got some things that've been used some back there." He gestured to a small alcove just beyond the line of dresses. "Mind how you go so's you don't get my merchandise dirty."

Tara slipped past the dresses with a soft sigh of longing. A table in the center of the space overflowed with all manner of well-used clothing. Discards from previous wagon trains when people died, or no longer needed the garments, no doubt. Many of the items were nearly as tattered as the clothing she wore, and all of it was just as dirty or even worse. She picked through the top few layers and found a gray dress with a frayed hem, but otherwise it was intact. It looked like it would fit or be just a bit too large on her.

She turned to call out to the shopkeeper only to find him standing directly behind her, a smirk on his face.

"H-how much for... this?" she asked, holding up the dress.

He rattled off a price that made her head spin. "Cash on the barrel," he added.

So much money for a dress that would be no more than a rag most places? "I... I actually... I was hoping we could work out a trade for some clothing... a few supplies..."

He shook his head, eyes flinty and lips thinned into a firm line. "Cash on the barrel," he repeated and jerked his thumb over his shoulder, pointing to a sign that read the same.

"I… see." Reluctantly, she shoved the dress back onto the heap. "I have to get a message to the law."

His eyes narrowed in suspicion. "Ain't got no way to get any message out."

She wasn't certain she believed him, but it was obvious he would not help her with anything. Tears stung her eyes as she pushed past the shopkeeper and walked into the main area.

A rumble rose from her stomach as she eyed a tray with some kind of jerky meat behind the counter. But a glance at the shopkeeper told her he would have no sympathy for her plight.

"Is there nothing I can do to earn some clothing… a little food?" she asked, knowing she was begging and beyond caring.

"No."

"But I don't have anywhere to go. I have no food…" Tears cascaded down her cheeks. "What will I do?"

"Wait for the next train through, I expect," he snapped. "Ask some folks that come along for food and clothing. Some might be accommodating."

"Wh-when will the next wagon train come?" she forced herself to ask.

"Can't say." He shrugged. "Could be today, might be next month."

Tara's heart sank, and she chewed her bottom lip.

A sly smile raised one corner of the shopkeeper's mouth. "Or there are always the trappers that come in… maybe one of them will buy you supplies and keep you."

She just stared him down and then sat by the stove. He didn't scare her. She'd faced down worse than that pompous… Her breath caught as she stilled her unmerciful thoughts. She would try to be the lady her mother had always said she should be at least, but it was hard. Very hard.

She wondered what the proprietor would say if she asked for a pair of trousers?

Oh, why had her mother died so young?

The door opened and two men in buckskins walked in. They were cleaner than she. They looked her over and kept walking as though they'd decided she wasn't worth their time. If her situation hadn't been so dire she would have laughed and loudly. For there was a time... But she forced those thoughts from her mind.

Would she even be fed here at the fort? Somehow she doubted it. At least she'd had water at the outside pump, so her immediate thirst had been quenched. But the thought of the next train being a month away made her body shake. It was still early in the season when not as many hit the trail west.

She watched the two men as they wandered the store and assessed her chances. Maybe she could handle them and keep them from touching her. Oh, if only she had her rifle, she'd just hunt for dinner. But no sense worrying over what she couldn't do anything about.

In a few more hours, dusk would be falling, and she'd see what she could do to find a place to sleep. If things hadn't happened so fast she would have at least taken supplies with her. Her gaze traveled the room, taking in the prices that were being charged for merchandise, and her mouth dropped open. If people paid that much for flour, then the owner could afford to give her a blanket, or at least let her choose from the pile of soiled clothing.

Some fort this had turned out to be. There wasn't a soldier to be seen. It was a trading post, nothing more. She'd wanted to alert the authorities, but there wasn't a way to do it from the "fort." Glancing out the window she saw two bedrolls and two horses. Would they hang a woman for stealing a horse? Maybe... and she wasn't willing to risk it. But surely a stolen bedroll was not worth pursuing.

She tiptoed out the door and filched the bedroll. She quickened her step and when she was out of sight of the store, she made a dash for the woods. She had to get through scrub and low brush to get to the forest's edge., she found a tree she could climb and scrambled up the trunk. She sat in the tree watching for the two men.

She'd already spent enough nights alone and frightened. At least she'd be warm now.

She realized that many folks failed to look up when they were searching for something. If she had a slingshot, she could get herself a bird to cook. She was so tired.

ZANDER RODE his horse next to Heath and Dawn, who were in the covered wagon. When Fort Bridger came into sight both Heath and Zander exchanged frowns. The place was little more than a small group of derelict cabins and a lean-to stable surrounded by a rickety fence with most of its sections lying flat to the ground. One stiff wind would likely flatten most of the buildings.

"That's a fort?" Dawn asked, her eyes wide with shock. "It's a good thing I married you, Heath. I doubt there would be much choice of men in that... Is it even a trading post?"

Two riders approached, pushing their mounts hard enough to raise a cloud of dust in their wake. Heath brought the wagon to a stop. The two men rode up to them and reined the horses in with abrupt yanks that had them neighing in protest.

"Did you see a girl with a bedroll?" The larger of the two asked as the swirling dust settled.

"Just a bedroll?" asked Zander. "That would have been an

odd sight. But no we didn't see anyone. Whoever you're looking for, she must have gone another way." He didn't like the fact that two men were looking for a girl, even though they seemed more interested in the bedroll they believed her to be carrying.

"Thanks." Without further interaction, they both turned their horses and spurred them into a gallop back the way they'd come.

Dawn laughed. "One horse was without a bedroll tied to the back of it."

Heath climbed down and turned to help his new wife down. He smiled at her as his hands lingered on her waist. Zander suppressed a twinge of irritation at the display.

"We'd best go talk to Harrison and see what supplies he wants us to get," Zander said.

"Will you be fine without me for a moment?" Heath asked his new wife.

Zander laughed. "I have it on good authority that Dawn can take care of herself. Let's go."

They walked out of Dawn's hearing. "She's not a child, you know."

"Zander, please don't give me advice. It's the fastest way for a fight to start."

"I suppose punching each other wouldn't be good for our friendship," Zander conceded.

"Sometimes I think we're making strides, then a bad memory comes back and paralyzes her. I knew that going in, and we've been praying on it. It's not that she doesn't trust me. I just don't know how to rid her of things the Indians did to her."

"And that is why I will never get married. As you can see I'm problem free. And I'm staying away from any women under twenty who will lie to get married."

Heath grinned. "Good idea."

THE TWO MEN searching for her were coming too close. Tara climbed higher into the tree. As long as she didn't fall they wouldn't be able to see her. She hoped.

A wagon train had arrived at Fort Bridger. Perhaps she might get lucky. Maybe someone on the train would take pity on her, or maybe someone needed help with children or cooking. She could work to pay her way if she found someone who needed her. Even as the thought formed in her mind, she knew it would be futile. She was alone and destitute. But she couldn't approach anyone at the fort. Were they planning to stay the night there or move on?

The two trappers were almost under her now. She stayed very still, holding her breath. She tried to close her eyes, but feared she would slip and fall.

"Why do you think that girl was alone?" the bigger one asked.

"Did you see how raggedy she looked? Let's just go. We're close enough to home I won't need the bedroll tonight anyway. Poor little mite, she'd best pray if she plans to spend the night out here alone." He looked around, and then he shrugged. "Let's ride."

Her choices became a choice of one. She needed to hide in a wagon. She wasn't sleeping outside tonight.

She climbed down, snagging her dress on a gnarly branch. Pulling it free caused another hole, and a sigh escaped. What did it matter? It was one of many now. There was only one way that wagon train would go, and she would have to go with it. She knew most folks wouldn't allow a single female to join them, let alone one without money, but if she could just find the right person… a widower, perhaps

The people on the train looked to be hitching up and loading their wagons. Now to get into one before they started to move. She bent to keep her body lowered and ran as fast as she could toward the fort.

She hid behind the store and waited. Two wagons we set apart with no one behind them. She slipped into the back of one and lay on her side behind a few stacked trunks. She ended up wedged in fairly tight, but wiggled and stretched, and pushed the trunks for a little more room.

The wagon swayed as the owners climbed onto the front bench, and Tara felt a rush a relief when a man yelled, "Haw!" The wagon lurched forward

It was an unbearably bumpy ride with the trunks banking against her. But she'd stay put and wait until they stopped for the night before she talked to the captain. They needed to be warned.

Her eyes grew heavy and the jolts became fewer as the wagon settled into a kind of lulling rocking. She must have fallen asleep. With a sharp gasp, she woke. The wagon wasn't moving. From the long shadows on the canvas, she could tell the sun would set in a few hours.

She tried to push the trunks back a bit but they wouldn't budge. Now what? She pushed again, grunting a bit with the effort. Finally, winded and growing anxious, she admitted there was nothing for it. She'd have to call for help and hope whoever found her didn't have a rifle.

ZANDER DROPPED some sticks and small branches he'd collected near the fire. Now that he felt secure that the plan he, Declan, and Heath had first made for a ranch together had changed none, he felt like a different person. He was even helpful. He snorted at the thought of how domesticated that sounded.

A soft sound gave him pause. He cocked his head and

listened. Then he took a few steps toward the back of the wagon and listened again. It almost sounded like an animal in pain. He took his gun out of the holster and climbed into the wagon. He listened again. His heart hardened, and he gripped his gun tighter. It wasn't an animal.

"Come on out with your hands up," he demanded leveling the gun on the stack of trunks to the side of the wagon.

"I'm stuck." the muffled voice cried.

Zander recoiled. Was that a female? "Stuck how?"

"The trunks are squishing me against the side of the wagon. Can you help me?"

He put his gun back into the holster and walked forward. He swung the bottom trunk out a bit and looked. Sure and it *was* a female. He pushed the trunks toward the center of the wagon. "Are you hurt?"

"A few bruises but it's nothing."

As she sat, a rolled-up blanket showed beneath her, and Zander nodded to it.

"That bedroll… that wouldn't be the one that was stolen is it?"

She paled. "It is. I thought I'd have to spend another night on the ground alone."

Zander narrowed his eyes as he held out his hand to help her up. "How long have you been out here?"

"I'd like to speak to your Captain. There's trouble a few days from here. I need to warn—" She broke off and sighed. "I'm Tara Carmichael."

"I'm Zander Leary." He jumped out of the wagon and helped Tara down. "Trouble, you say? Let's go find the captain."

People of the wagon party all stared at them as they went in search of Captain London. To Zander's surprise, he was drinking coffee at his own wagon for a change.

"What's going on here?" he asked.

With a fleeting glance at Zander, Miss. Tara Carmichael began speaking, her voice desperate, her gestures wild. "Sir, everyone from my train was murdered. I went to the fort but the man there wouldn't give me any help, so I hid in one of the wagons. I have had nothing to eat in a few days, and frankly I'm scared."

"Zander, see what you can rustle up. Someone must have their supper ready. And you, Miss.... What might your name be?"

Zander didn't have to go far. The wagon behind the captain's already had a cook fire going with food heating. After he explained the situation, the man and his wife happily provided a plate with beans and bread. Zander strode back to Captain London's wagon, and Tara smiled at him as he handed the plate to her.

"Did you see how many?" the captain asked.

"I was indisposed at first, away from the others. When I heard shouting, I lay flat on my stomach and tried to see through the tall grass. There was running and screaming and the men yelling in triumph. They even took a few scalps. It was so hard not to scream and run toward the wagons to help, but I didn't have a gun on me. They slaughtered everyone I knew. Then they rummaged through the wagons and seemed mad that they didn't find whatever they thought they'd find. I wish I could have closed my eyes and put my hands over my ears. I didn't move until it got dark, and I'm glad I didn't. They came back and went through the wagons again. They left again, still angry. I snuck away and made my way to the fort." She wiped her tears away and sighed.

"So, it wasn't Indians?" Captain London sounded disbelieving.

"Not any that I saw. I saw at least four men and they were white. I tried to report it at the fort, but the storekeeper said they didn't have any way of reporting it, no authorities there.

The man there wasn't accommodating. I guess if you don't have money he wasn't interested."

"The bedroll," Captain London murmured. "Where were you headed before all this happened?"

"I was on my way to Oregon with my father. We were coming from the Smokey Mountains, and we were excited to homestead in Oregon. We were thrilled to build a new house and learn about a new land. I guess it's just me now…" Her voice trailed off as her shoulders slumped. "I don't know what I'm supposed to do now."

"Zander, will you take her back to the wagon?" London asked, but it was really more of an order. "Harrison has asked for the next available wagon for his growing family. Meaning you, Heath, and Declan. I have extra supplies I can donate, and maybe one of the women will find a dress or two for… for… I didn't even get your name."

"Tara Carmichael, sir."

"Tara, I'd appreciate it if you stayed in the wagon. If any of the men from the raid see you alive and recognize you, they won't be happy they've left a witness. We need to sort a few things out, but you can trust Zander and anyone he introduces you to."

"Thank you."

Zander tried to get back to the wagon with no one noticing, but plenty of the folks in the wagon train saw them.

"Who is she and how is she traveling with us?" Patty Mince asked rather boldly.

Before long, a crowd began to gather and Tara backed up against Zander. Zander groaned. Everyone had to pry into everyone else's business on this journey.

"Tara here got separated from her party, and we're taking her with us to meet up with those who took Sublette's Cutoff in the hope she'll be reunited with her group. Captain London asked me to keep her in the wagon for now."

He wanted to laugh. Almost all of them looked as though they didn't believe him. Too bad. He escorted her back to where he found her. Heath and Dawn were building a fire together. It looked to be taking a long time since Heath had to kiss Dawn on the cheek every few seconds. They jumped apart when he and Tara approached.

"Meet Tara, our new passenger," Zander said.

Heath and Dawn both nodded to Tara and then stared at him for an explanation.

"First, I need to get her into the wagon and then I'll explain." He put his hands around her tiny waist and lifted into the wagon. He could have sworn she frowned at him.

"We're not to let her be seen, though most of the camp has seen her by now. I'll explain when everyone gets here."

Dawn appeared perplexed. "I'll gather the rest." She hurried off.

"You can tell me," Heath coaxed.

Zander laughed and nodded toward the approaching group of people. "Here they come." He waited while Harrison and Cora, Luella and Declan joined them. "Tara is inside the wagon."

Tara nodded from the back of the wagon.

"She saw her whole party slaughtered a few days ago and has been on her own. Captain London asked that she stay hidden since she's the only witness. She hid out in our wagon because needed help but also because she wanted to warn us."

Everyone stared at him taking it all in. Cora was the first into the wagon, followed by Luella and Dawn. Essie—Cora and Harrison's baby—cried, and Cora just put her hands out and waited for Harrison to put Essie into her arms.

"The bedroll?" Declan asked.

Zander nodded. "She was traveling with her father and went

to take care of personal needs in the tall grass when it happened. They were white men, and they were looking for something. They came back hours after they killed everyone to take another look. Tara stayed in the same place until nighttime, and she's been walking and hiding since it happened. She hadn't had any food. I managed to get her a plate of beans. She did get water at the fort. She has nothing except, now, the bedroll."

"Why didn't she stay and get help from the man at the fort?" Heath asked.

"He told her he couldn't get any messages out. Her clothes are torn to shreds, and she was hungry. What type of person turns his back on another in need?" Zander shook his head. "What? I have compassion and can even be nice occasionally."

Harrison's lips twitched. "You can't blame us for being surprised is all. How many men are we talking about?"

"She saw four men but is sure there were more. They even scalped some of the dead."

"Trying to make it look as though Indians had done it?" Declan asked, his voice laced with anger.

"If she saw who did it, she's in danger. We need to guard her at night," Harrison said.

Heath frowned. "How are we going to do that, watch the cattle, and sleep next to our wives?"

Declan laughed. "It's not easy being newly wed on this trip."

"It's not just that," Heath protested. "Dawn has nightmares."

"We'll draw up a schedule, and Dawn can bunk with Tara on nights you have guard duty. Any of our wives can double up. Have a feeling we'll all be pulling extra guard duty to keep us all safe," Harrison said.

They all turned toward the wagon when they heard

laughter. "A hen party?" Zander furrowed his brow. "I thought there'd be tears."

Harrison nodded. "That might come next with Cora and Luella both expecting."

Declan grimaced. "Why?"

"Pregnant women cry a lot," Harrison told him.

"It'll be a long trip if that happens," Declan said.

Harrison smiled. "Yes it will."

CHAPTER TWO

*T*ara tried repeatedly to fall asleep. But her thoughts were too full of what had happened and of where she now was. If only she could get her brain to just stop. When she closed her eyes, she saw the people of her wagon party being killed. Her father was dead, she'd seen him fall. She could still hear the screams during the attack and see all the blood. It was too disturbing to relive, but her mind wouldn't let it go.

Sleeping in the wagon was a nice twist of fate. She had fully expected to sleep outside on the stolen bedroll. But everyone had been very kind to her, especially the handsome man named Zander. His eyes were a vivid blue and his hair was dark. He was tall but not as brawny as his friend Declan.

Men were never interested in her except in one way. She was too much of a tomboy. She could do all the chores a woman needed to do but she also could do anything a man could do. She loved to hunt. The woods, any woods, were where'd she'd rather be.

Were her belongings still in the wagon? She had always worn buckskins until this trip. But her father insisted she wear dresses, behave more ladylike. It had been hard to talk to other women, though. She wasn't interested in the latest styles or recipes. She'd rather set her rabbit traps or prepare the skins to sell at the trading post. There probably weren't many men in Oregon who would want a wife such as her. Would she feel safe enough to make a life on her own?

She knew how to survive but as far as manners went; she knew only the bare basics—as to the rest; she was clueless. Shuffling noises rose from outside as someone rolled under the wagon. The guard shift must have changed. She didn't want to be a bother. All she needed was a rifle and a hunting knife and she could pull her weight. She knew as long as she stayed with this party, though, that would never happen. She'd be useful, at least. She could drive a wagon. She might look puny, but she was strong.

She liked the women she'd met, but if she had to pick one she'd pick Dawn. She was a survivor. Tara could tell by the look in her eyes.

Finally, the sun was due to rise, and she opened the canvas in the back of the wagon a bit. A burst of refreshing, cool morning air blew in, and her heart gave a pang. Morning had been her father's favorite time of day. If only her father was with her now. He'd been her only friend, and it was as if part of her was missing. He expected her to marry someday, but she wasn't sure who she was supposed to marry. Besides, she didn't need a man in her life.

She was used to keeping busy and sitting idle didn't feel right. She could have had a fire going and breakfast made by now. Eventually, the other women were up, and Luella and Dawn needed things from their trunks. Tara was just in the way. Perhaps it wasn't the best of ideas to stay, but what other choice did she have?

Cora came with her baby girl and handed Tara a dress. "This should fit until I can make you more."

"Thank you, Cora." Tara unfolded the dress and found herself surprised at how pretty it was.

"Luella and Dawn are good with a needle too, so we should have you outfitted in no time."

"It's a lot of trouble to go to."

"We don't mind. Helping each other makes our lives and our travels less difficult."

Tara smiled. "I've never worked with women before. It's always just been me and my Pa. So, what are the rules? Do we all try to get along? Do we vote on which way to do things? Do I do more work since I'm the new person?"

Cora's lips twitched. "I don't think there are rules. You try to get along with everyone and be respectful. If we think we're right, we don't tell someone else they are wrong. We explain why we believe our way is better. We're all from different backgrounds, and we've learned a lot from one another. I never had female friends either, but I've found I rather like it."

"I guess I'll watch while I'm stuck in here and try to learn."

Cora leaned in and patted Tara's hand. "Oh, my. Could you hold Essie for a moment?" Cora didn't wait for a reply. She just handed the baby to Tara and ran toward the woods.

Tara and Essie eyed each other. "I once had a bobcat. I raised him from a kitten."

Essie watched her. "I do believe you are the first human baby I've ever held. So what do we do next?"

Essie was cooing and smiling until she wasn't. Her cried pierced the quiet of the morning. Now what? Tara was out of her element. "Shh, baby."

Zander climbed through the front and sat in the wagon. "Here give her to me."

Tara quickly handed him the wailing child. "I didn't do anything to her."

Zander smiled. "Essie, what's with all this noise my sweet, sweet, colleen?" He kissed her cheek before he laid her against his chest, her head on his shoulder. She quieted and suddenly seemed quite content.

"I guess you and Essie have met before."

"We're old friends. Do you remember where the attack happened?"

"Yes, we took the Sublette Cutoff, and we stopped at Thomas Fork before Bear River. We rested a few days, and the group who took the Fort Bridger route caught up. We rested with them for a day, and then we continued. It's beautiful along the Bear. At least it was." She glanced down at her hands. The shock of what had happened was being replaced with horror and loss.

"We have folks to meet at Thomas Fork too. I'm so sorry. It must have been horrible to watch and then terrifying to have to lie so still looking at all the death and destruction. You want to look away but you can't, your kin are there dead. After, when you realize you can go you do so but leaving is hard too. Panic sets in, where are you to go? Now you're in danger and have to hide. Part of you wishes you had died too and another part is so grateful to God that you lived. Tragedies happen in many places. Some say it strengthens you, but I never found that to be true. I just found it to be an unjustified tragedy that can't be avenged and it's in my heart at all times."

She lifted her head and stared at him. "That's exactly how I feel. I'm sorry for your loss but I feel comforted that someone knows how I feel. You must tell me your story sometime."

He patted Essie on the back. "Perhaps. It's a long story."

Cora poked her head in. "Oh, Zander, I didn't know you were in here. Essie sure does love you." She reached her hands out, and Zander placed the child into her arms. "I'm sorry I ran out so fast but morning sickness got the better of me." She smiled as she cuddled the baby near and walked away.

"I've never held a baby before."

"You did well. I'm going to slip out before I get caught in here alone and have to marry you."

She watched him leave. Have to get married? What was that all about?

THERE WERE no secrets or privacy to be had. They'd been traveling four days, and he was getting a hard stare from most of the women. Everyone seemed to know that Tara was riding with them and that he visited her. It was nothing but a traveling community you couldn't leave for months and months.

It was getting late in the day, and the plan was to get to Thomas Fork and meet the others. Many speculated on whether they were alive. Zander didn't care. Cora had a friend who had gone the way of the waterless dust.

As soon as they sighted the wagons, an air of happiness seemed to float from wagon to wagon. They formed the familiar circle near the water. Many scrambled to see how well the others had fared.

Cora ran when she spotted Sally and Rod Waverly. Sally broke down into tears while Cora held her.

Zander watched for a specific three, though he would have been fine if they didn't come back. Troublemakers; Chuck Klass, Eddie Connors, and the Scout Tom Simps. And there they were. Eddie was gaunt and limping. Chuck Klass had but one ox pulling his wagon and Tom was lying on a bedroll near a fire. Many others looked as though they had suffered. It didn't look as though the cutoff was worth it.

Their livestock looked exhausted and poorly after resting for four days.

Zander and Harrison exchanged worried glances. He hoped no one would think they would get their hands on any of Harrison's live stock.

Captain London stood on his familiar crate and called for all to come close. "Looks like most made it. We'll be here for two more nights. Meanwhile we need to be extra diligent. A wagon train not too far from here was attacked."

"Indians?" someone asked.

"White men wiped out most of the party. They were brutal, as brutal as Indians. We'll take the time to dig graves when we get there. I don't know if there are any wagons that were left undamaged. We have the witness with us, and no one will touch a wagon. She has first right if anything is still there. Carry your weapons and no one should wander off. I will double the guards. One more thing, the people who took Sublette's Cutoff were warned about how hard it would be. Do not put anyone on the spot by asking for their livestock. Your decision, your consequences.

"It's that sorry excuse of a scout's fault! He never found us food or water!" Eddie yelled.

The scout, Tom Simps struggled to stand. "You were told there wouldn't be water, and if you needed food, you should have gone to Bridger's Fort. You refused to travel at night until I finally left you behind. You have been nothing but trouble from the day you joined our group!" Tom staggered and a few men helped him back down to his bedroll.

Captain London stared Eddie down. "I spoke with each of you taking that cutoff. I told you what to expect. You added more than a day by not traveling at night. Have you no care for animals? Don't you dare ask Harrison for help. Not after all you put his wife through. You might have to see if someone will share their wagon with you!"

The captain then scanned the crowd. "Every man will take a turn at guard duty. A few of you paid Tom to not put you on the schedule. That will happen no more. Zander, I'll need you to help me make a schedule seeing as you pull the most duty of anyone."

Zander nodded. It was nice to be treated like an equal. He'd always just been Declan and Heath's friend.

"Where is this survivor? How do we know it's not a trap?" Chuck Klass demanded.

"It's not a trap and that's all you need to know," the captain said.

"I'll go from wagon to wagon and hunt her out like the liar she is!"

Harrison stepped forward. "Why is it you give no one the benefit of the doubt? The young lady watched her father and everyone on her wagon train killed. If I find you near her—"

"Another stray for you and your group? We shouldn't have to put up with you and your questionable women!"

Reverend Paul stepped between the men. "Let's all be thankful that no one died on our way here to Thomas Fork. It's a time for joy, not a time for violence or harsh words."

"I still have the right to question her!"

Captain London Held his hands up. "No one will disturb her or mention her." He got down from his crate and walked to his wagon.

Harrison, Declan, Heath, and Zander stood shoulder to shoulder and stared Chuck down. He finally grunted and left.

"I HEARD SOME BUT NOT ALL," Tara had her head and shoulders out of the canvas waiting for them to come back.

"Not too much to hear," Declan said.

"The ones who traveled the cutoff aren't happy. I guess they had a hard time of it," Heath explained as he sat on a crate and pulled Dawn down onto his lap. It was impossible to miss the love between them. All of them actually.

Tara wasn't schooled in the ways of married folks. Harrison treated Cora and Essie as if he'd protect them to the very end. Declan's gaze followed Luella and there was a look in his eyes and Tara wished someone would gaze at her the same way. Heath and Dawn were harder to read. She startled easily and stiffened when Heath first touched her but then a loving smile crossed her face, and they would hold each other as though no matter what they were one.

Zander frowned a lot, but he seemed to ignore all the evidence of love. Though she heard one of the men talking about Zander routinely making himself scarce during the evenings. They speculated he was meeting someone.

She wasn't so sure. He never mentioned a woman, and he didn't seem to be in a hurry to meet anyone, but she'd only known him for a fortnight. She valued his friendship the most. She heard horses and ducked back inside the wagon. She had a bad feeling. She gathered a few supplies and put them in a flour sack. The bed roll was ready to go with her too.

"Come on," Zander whispered to her from the bench in the wagon's front.

Nodding, she grabbed the bedroll and the sack. She climbed out the front, and keeping low, they made a run for the woods. They went far enough not to be seen but close enough to watch.

"Chuck Klass," Zander growled when one man pointed to the wagon she'd just been in.

"Turncoat," she spat.

"Are those the men?"

"Only the one on the roan. The others I haven't seen before. What if they start shooting?"

He took her hand and led her to a rather large tree. "Declan saw them far off, and we hid some rifles and ammunition here. There's food and water too."

He checked to make sure the rifle was loaded and handed it to her. She grabbed up the shells and put them in her pocket. Then she grabbed another rifle. Staying down she crawled toward the edge of the woods.

Zander was right behind her, and they lay side by side ready to shoot. "You really know how to use those?"

Turning her head she nodded. "I hunted most days. No matter what it took, we had to eat."

"Aye, I had to eat too, but I didn't have a rifle. I'm surprised I wasn't sent away on a convict ship. But I was lucky and didn't get caught. Fortune smiled on me one day, and they hired me on a ship to America. Here I was able to find a job and pay my way."

"Look, Zander they are going through the wagon. Why hasn't anyone stopped them?" She shivered. "We could easily pick them off one by one just the two of us."

"We can't hear what's happening, and I'm not for killing until I know the whole story."

"You're probably right. What do you think they've been saying?"

"I wish I knew."

Just having Zander at her side gave her the confidence she needed. She knew he'd defend her just as she would for him. There wasn't anything to find in the wagon but having a killer in the camp wasn't right. It was downright dangerous.

"Maybe I should just shoot the one on the roan. I *did* see him kill people."

Zander's lips twitched.

"I don't see what's so amusing. Don't I have the right to avenge my father?"

"I'm just afraid you'll end up strung up. We'll wait and see what they wanted and let everyone know the tall man on the roan is a killer. I'd love to know what story he is telling the others."

"Story? As in *I* killed everyone?"

"Could be." He reached over and squeezed her hand lightly. "They'll be gone soon enough."

CHAPTER THREE

Zander waited until it was dark before he smuggled Tara back into the wagon. The men had been gone for hours, but for some reason he had the feeling they were watching. "How much would you mind posing as a boy?"

Her smile lit up her face. "Bring me some trousers and a hat. I've had to pretend to be a boy many times. There weren't many females where we lived, and Pa was afraid one of the men might carry me off."

"You pulled it off in the daylight?"

"Sure did, why?"

"It's just that you're kind of pretty, and I certainly wouldn't mistake you for a boy."

She turned red. "I scrub dirt on my face and clothes. Chewin' on tobacco helps too. That keeps the women away. My life has differed greatly from yours. But I wouldn't have changed it for all the silk dresses in the world. I am hoping my buckskins are still in the wagon, but I doubt it."

He shook his head. "I can't imagine it."

"Are you in that wagon with that killer?"

Zander grimaced. It was the thorn in his side, Eddie.

Zander poked his head out of the wagon. "Mind your own business. Your verbal abuse toward Cora hasn't made you any friends. You need not know everything. Besides, she's not a killer."

"You'll be forced to marry the little tramp. What is it with all of you and your arranged marriages? Not a courted match in the bunch." He snickered. "Not that it matters. Now you'll be stuck with that little thief."

"Eddie, I'm never getting married. I don't want a wife, ever. Goodnight."

Zander turned back to Tara and smiled. "I'd best get to sleep under the wagon."

"Is he right? Were Harrison, Declan and Heath all forced to marry?"

"Yes. Goodnight." He climbed out of the front of the wagon, laid out his bedroll and crawled under the wagon, his weapons by his side.

They *had* all been forced to marry, yet they seemed fine with it. But he didn't need a millstone around his neck. Looking out for himself had taken all he had in Ireland. He never wanted to bring a child into the world either. Children were too vulnerable, and awful things happened. A frown drew in his brows. He'd better spend less time with Tara. He'd rather leave the wagon train then get hitched to some female. There were more men than women out here. Tara would find someone. He rolled over and went to sleep.

He woke to a rustling noise, and then a shot rang out above him. He rolled out from under the wagon and looked inside. One of the men who'd been there that morning was lying on top of Tara. Blood was splattered everywhere, and she was frantically trying to get out from under the body.

Zander vaulted into the wagon, pulled the dead body off her and carried her out. She stood there staring at the wagon in silence. Zander pulled his gun out in case there were others. He turned in a circle searching.

The shot had woken most of the party and Captain London came running. "What happened? Where were the guards? Tara, are you hurt?"

She shook her head. "It's not my blood." Her eyes appeared so big on her face. Fearing she would faint, Zander grabbed a crate for her to sit on. "It was one of the men who were here earlier. Not the one on the roan. They're probably watching me now. I brought danger to you. I'm so sorry."

People began peering around and pointing their guns toward the outside of the wagon circle.

"Everyone stay put," ordered London. "I want the men to grab their guns and check the perimeter and make sure the guards are fine. Check your own wagons too! Don't shoot each other!" The captain sat on one crate and sighed heavily. "Dawn, could you please make some coffee? It will be a long night or an extremely early morning."

"I'd be happy to." She wrapped her shawl around herself and got the fire built up before she made the coffee and put it on the fire to boil.

Luella looked in the wagon then promptly ran off and was sick.

"I'm sorry," Tara said. "It's my fault. I'll get started on cleaning the wagon now."

She stood and as she tried to climb into the wagon, Zander pulled her into his arms and carried her to Cora's tent. He entered and laid Tara down on the bed next to Cora who was nursing Essie.

"Sorry to invade your privacy, Cora. I needed a place for Tara to lie down." He walked out of the tent.

"I SHOULDN'T BE in here. I smell like blood. I'll leave." Tara shuffled toward the tent opening. She had no intention of staying put. She had brought these people danger, and she would not be part of any forced marriage. Who did these people think they were forcing others to marry? It made no sense at all to her.

"I will take Essie into our wagon. Would you like to join us? There is water in the basin by the trunk, and I have dresses in there too that you could try."

"Thanks, Cora, but I'm fine right here, at least for the moment. I would like to clean up though."

Cora and Essie weren't gone for more than a half hour when there were more gunshots.

Tara ran out of the tent wearing wool trousers and a shirt five sizes two big. She had a beat up hat on and a pistol in her waistband. She used a piece of rope to keep her pants up. Zander was right about her dressing as a boy. Hopefully Harrison wouldn't mind her borrowing his clothes. She stopped and took in everything around her. People were rushing to the other side of the camp.

After grabbing a bit of dirt, she rubbed it on her face. Then she hurried to Cora's wagon and found it empty. Puzzled, she went to the wagon she had slept in. Dawn was putting everything that had blood on it in a pile.

"What happened to the others? Who is shooting?" Tara could hardly catch her breath she was so upset.

"Tara?" She squinted at her, a frown wrinkling her forehead. "I think they spotted deer. I assume that explains the gunshots. Cora is in the tent with Luella. Luella is expecting and having a hard time keeping anything down. Now, tell me why you are dressed in… Are those Harrison's clothes?"

"I figured if I left, y'all would be safe. Traveling as a boy is much easier than traveling as a female. I want—I need—I want to gun down the men who killed the people on the wagon train I traveled on. I need to know why they killed everyone."

"You said they searched your train's wagons twice?" She shook her head. "They must have been looking for something in particular. Was anyone carrying anything valuable like guns or money? I'm just so sorry you've had to go through it. Why don't you have a cup of coffee? Bet the captain has more questions for you." Dawn smiled and went back to cleaning.

She'd planned to just leave, but she hadn't thought everything through. She needed to stay and keep Cora, Dawn, and Luella safe. And the baby. Her eyes watered. There had been children on the train she'd been on. Innocent babes. What were those men looking for? What could it be?

And they had come right for her this time. How did they know who she was and what she saw? That could only mean one thing. There was a snake in the grass, and she was going to find out who. She watched people walking around. A few started cook fires and had coffee on to boil. Pulling her hat down, she concealed more of her face. She looked at people from under the brim. Almost all of them wore frowns. There was also fear in some women's eyes.

It was all because of her. How far away was Fort Hall? The only thing she knew was she had heard the water would start tasting worse as they went along toward Soda Springs. Some she'd met as she traveled said they liked the water. She couldn't abide its sulfur smell. It was drinkable and usable and perhaps she shouldn't have complained.

She waved a hand in front of her face trying to get the mosquitoes away. They were unusually thick in number. It was best to stay near the fire and away from the water to reduce the pesky bugs that bit. The swarms seemed bigger than before but she hadn't had time for sitting then.

"Tara? Is that you?" Declan asked. "The captain would like to talk to you in his tent."

She glanced up at him. "Tent?"

"Are those Harrison's clothes?" He waved a hand as if to tell her to ignore his question. "It's a big tent and others are already in there talking about the man that was killed. I guess they have a couple of questions."

"No. I won't go. It'll just lead to a lynching, mine to be exact."

"Why would you think that?"

"I've seen people gather after a death, especially a shooting, and the next thing you know there's a hanging." She tilted her head. Surely he knew this.

"They just want more information so we can protect ourselves. Come on."

"Tara, the captain—" Zander nodded to them both. "Let's go."

She wasn't being given a choice. She might as well get it over with.

"You don't seem surprised to see her in Harrison's clothes," Declan commented.

"It's a great disguise, though Harrison is a big man. She should have asked Heath for some of his."

Declan laughed. "She should have asked for yours."

"I *was* small from starvation, but this trip has made me filled out and strong."

They exchanged some knowing look, and Declan nodded.

Declan held the tent flap open. She took Zander's hand before entering. By the way people zeroed in on their hands it had been a mistake, and she let go.

"Tara, come take a seat." The captain gestured for her to sit on a crate in the same area where he was sitting on a much larger one.

"You're not a judge are you?"

"No, but I make the decisions while we are traveling."

She wrinkled her nose. "Ever send a person to the hangman?"

Captain London's eyes widened, then he smiled. "Not yet."

Tara swallowed hard and glanced away.

"Tara, did you know the man who was killed?"

"No, only that he was with the man who rode the roan. The man who rode the roan was one of the men I saw killing people. I stayed hidden and wish I could have closed my eyes but I couldn't. I saw it happen."

She heard murmurs and realized there were over ten men in the tent. Her nerves must have gotten the best of her. Usually she was observant of her surroundings.

"Did he say anything to you? Did he draw his gun?"

She gave a decisive nod. "He drew his gun, and I heard him pull back the hammer. I turned from my side and shot him before he could shoot me. I was also afraid for whoever was under the wagon. A bullet can go through wood you know."

"Zander, you were the one sleeping under the wagon, weren't you?"

"Yes, and I'm glad Tara thought of me under there." A smile tugged at one corner of his mouth,

"Miss. Carmichael, was everyone on your wagon train killed?"

"I believe so. No one was alive, but I don't know if anyone was able to sneak away. I didn't see anyone. It felt cowardly to watch, to not try to help, but I would only have been killed along with them."

The captain nodded. "You did the right thing. Tell me, do you know anyone on this wagon train? I mean from before the killing?"

"That's been puzzling me. I haven't seen anyone I recognize, but the killers knew I was here. Either someone told them or they planned to kill all of you too. But why start with just me?" She lifted her shoulders and let them fall. "Maybe they thought I knew something. I don't rightly know what, but something very strange is going on."

London gave her an assessing stare. "Are those Harrison's clothes?"

The crowd laughed.

"Yes, sir. I didn't steal them. I'm borrowing them." She narrowed her eyes.

"It's a good way to make them think you left us. If they're still watching, that is. Maybe they didn't get enough cash and are planning to wipe us out next. You may have saved us, Tara. No hangings today. Everyone, let's get ready to go. I want to put a few miles between us and those men."

She was first out of the tent, and she kept walking. They must think her simple minded. Why hadn't Declan told her that there would not be a hanging? Abruptly, she stopped and stared at the Bear River. Because she hadn't given him a chance. She was worse than her pa. He'd always jumped on things before finding out all the facts.

Turning, she watched some of the women. Most looked very feminine. Perhaps rubbing dirt on her face was a bit much. She just didn't know. She felt more relaxed in her borrowed clothes but what did a man think when he saw her?

The mosquitoes got to be too much and after waving her arms this way and that she headed for the wagon.

CHAPTER FOUR

They had been up one side of a mountain and down another. It had been an exhausting day, and Zander could see the tension building inside Tara. The camp should be another few miles ahead, and he didn't relish seeing and burying dead people.

"I never did ask what about the animals?"

Tara was quiet for a moment. "They were driven away. Sorry, I had forgotten that part. They rounded them up and drove them off. That adds at least four additional men. I had to walk all the way to the Fort Bridger because there wasn't a horse to be had. I was just glad there was water most of the way. How could I have forgotten?"

"You'd just seen people you knew brutally murdered. It's amazing you knew the way back to the fort."

"I can track anything. I'm a crack shot too. I'm good with a knife, and I hit what I aim for."

"You're talented."

"Yes," she sighed. "Men aren't looking for those types of talents. I've observed the camp, and the women with the best men wear dresses and keep their hair up. They don't seem to question their husbands. They are hardworking, and they seem to be able to make their man happy with the slightest of touches. They have set chores too. Men hunt, take care of the animals and the wagon, carry water and a few even gather wood. Men drive most of the wagons though a few women take the reins. It's interesting to watch and hard to understand."

"Surely you noticed things that way with your party."

Tara shrugged. "There weren't many women. I think one wife with children and then there was a wagon full of women my pa wouldn't allow me near. Personally, I thought they should have put on more clothes so the mosquitoes didn't get to them."

Zander wanted to laugh, but he held it in, knowing she'd be insulted. She sure was naïve. Her father hadn't done her any favors keeping her isolated on the mountain. Cora, Luella, and Dawn all tried to be friendly, but it was almost as though Tara didn't know how to act. Now he knew she didn't have a clue. That bit of information was bound to smooth a few ruffled feathers. Not that she hadn't wanted to be included; she just didn't know how to say yes. There was plenty of time yet for her to learn what she needed to find a husband. She'd be an asset to the right man. Her eyes were pools of chocolate, and her blond hair had a silky appearance. He often wondered what it would feel like. As far as dressing like a man, it was a good thing she did have Harrison's big shirt on. There was no real way to hide her curves.

He pulled on the reins and brought the wagon to a stop a bit away from the others. The wagons from Tara's train sat in the distance like an old ghost town with canvases ripped and blowing in the wind.

"I see it. Part of me wants to ride right by, but part of me had to see if anything of my pa is left." Her words quavered at the end.

"We'll circle with our party and then go look."

By the time they were situated and they had unhitched the animals, many people had already left for the empty wagons.

"I feel as though they don't have a right to be there. Look they are going through people's things. They don't even know who those things belonged to. Oh, Zander someone is pillaging my wagon."

They hurried forward, and Zander called out to the two drovers in her wagon. They looked sheepish and left the wagon empty-handed.

A single shot had everyone standing still. "Back away, and there had better not be anything in your hands or pockets," shouted Captain London. "You're all behaving like a wake of buzzards."

People had put what they wanted into piles for themselves. Zander could feel Tara's rage building. He took her hand and gently squeezed it.

"Tara, please come and show me exactly what you saw happen," Captain London called as he gestured for her to join him and his scout, Oscar. "Do you think you could walk me through it?"

"Wh-where are the bodies?"

"I had a group of trusted volunteers ride ahead of us and take care of it. I'll show you where your pa is when we're done." He sighed. "At least I think it's your pa. He had a leather bracelet around his wrist with the name Patrick Carmichael carved across it."

She nodded as a feeling of numbness crept over her. "I made that for him for Christmas when I was only thirteen."

Captain London's mouth thinned until it was only a flat line as he nodded. "I'm sorry, Miss. Carmichael."

"Thank you, Captain."

She walked to one wagon. "It was here I saw the first man

die." She gestured to a distant field. "I was over there in the grass when I heard gunshots. The murderers didn't make any type of cry they just attacked before people could reach for their rifles. Then panic started. Many tried to run, but they were caught. They used knives mostly. One man used a bow and arrow, but he was white. They were all white." She walked on to another wagon.

"Mrs. Parsons was inside with her four children. There hadn't been a sound from them but suddenly there was crying and screaming. Then it was silent again, but the canvas was covered in red. My pa was standing right here with a hatchet in one hand and his rifle in another. He'd always been good in a fight, but the person he was fighting didn't kill him. Someone shot him in the back. There was such a look of shock on his face. I could see it, even from far away. The last to die, I think, was the wagon master. They kept yelling at him to tell them the truth, and the man on the roan horse shot him in the head."

She stared dry-eyed into the distance. "They went through the wagons like I said, and they left, but they came back. I was still lying in the tall grass when they came back. I thought for sure they knew I was alive. I was both wise and a coward that day."

Zander turned her toward him and pulled her against his body, putting her head on his shoulder. He hadn't realized she was taller than most. He felt the heat from the stares of the others on him, but he didn't care. He had a feeling she'd had little comforting in her life.

"Thank you, Tara. Which wagon is yours?"

She pointed it out.

"Come I'll show you the grave." The captain turned to Oscar. "Don't allow anyone in the wagons until after Tara has a chance to take what she wants first and tell them to get rid of those ridiculous piles. I won't have her intimidated into not taking something that she wants."

He walked to a space near the forest.

"Someone carved his name on a cross. There are still good people in this world." She kneeled down and bowed her head in prayer.

Zander heard a lot of griping about how long she was taking. He needed to stay calm and not let his temper show. It was hard to rein himself in but he did it. Though he glared at the more vocal people.

Tara began to stand and Zander helped her up. "Captain, I believe it would be more respectful for Tara to go through the wagons without an audience."

"I concur! Everyone back to their wagons!"

The grumbling was loud as people walked back to the wagons.

"Thank you, Captain. Zander, would you come with me?"

Both men nodded.

HER HEART WAS heavy as she approached her wagon. She didn't expect much to be there. It looked to be in good shape, though. She stopped short and stared at it. Then she took a few steps and vaulted into the wagon. It was a bit of a mess and it had an odor of rotting food but she didn't see anything missing, except for her pa. His pipe lay on the floor and she picked it up, smelling it. She could see him sitting by the fire smoking and the memory both gave her joy and heartbreak. She put it in her pocket.

"If we can get the rotten food out, I'd like to drive my own wagon. I'd need some oxen but I can pay..." She looked for a secret drawer at the bottom of the bench. She had to take out many tools to get to it. *Please God, let it still be here.*

She opened the drawer and then sat down and cried.

"Tara it's fine. We might be able to work something out with Harrison. He has extra oxen with him, and I have my wages."

Tara smiled through her tears. "You are so sweet. You don't even know you offered me your future. All the money is there. My pa and I didn't need to spend much money, but we'd made plenty. There were a lot of trappers in the group." Shaking her head, she gulped in some air. "Maybe that was what they were after. I bet there is a fortune to be had inside these wagons. Come on, I'm supposed to go from wagon to wagon and see what I want."

By the time she was done, she had enough money to be one of the richest in Oregon. She also took supplies and things for the women who had been so kind to her. She hoarded all yarn, yard goods and anything else they could use to make things. Even though there weren't many women, there was a surprising amount of yarn, material, flour sacks and needles. She also took some extra pots, pans, quilts and candles. The best treasure was the amount of clean buck-skins she gathered. To anyone else it looked as though she hardly took a thing but she had all she needed and more.

"Tell the captain the rest can come. I will clean my wagon out and then talk to Harrison about the oxen. I bet they have more at Fort Hall. Just imagine, Zander, I have the means to make a future for myself."

"Are you going to build a big house?"

She shook her head. "No, I have no need for big or grand. I want a log house a little bigger than we had and maybe a water pump."

Warmth stole over her as she watched him walk away. She knew he wanted to be a bachelor, and she respected his wishes. And maybe he would find the right woman someday. Maybe he'd bump into his intended on the wooden walk or in a store. She had picked up bits and pieces about his life in Ireland. He'd been on his own when he was far too young. It sounded like a hard life.

She would ease his burden of looking out for her. She gathered her strength and cleaned the wagon out. She couldn't watch as the others grabbed whatever they could find. Things shouldn't go to waste but there had to be a more civilized way.

She scrubbed the inside of the wagon, and the foul smell left. She felt him behind her but she didn't turn. She didn't want him to think he wasn't able to surprise her. It made her smile.

"Tara?"

She turned, and there was his big smile. He was made for smiling. He had dimples and deep smile lines on his face. Looking at him you'd never know he'd ever been sad.

She saw he clutched her father's rifle and hatchet in his hands. She took them both and stared at them. She caressed the rifle. It had been her father's constant companion. After touching every inch she examined the hatchet. Her father was as skilled as any warrior in a fight. She never needed to feel fear when her father was near.

Her eyes pooled as her gaze met Zander's. "I thank you. You have no idea what having his weapons mean to me. I also thank you or making that fine marker for his grave. You're one of the best men I know Zander Kennedy. I'm proud to be your friend. If you ever need help I'd be more than glad to help you."

She held out her hand out to shake his. He always made her heart beat faster when they touched. "Friends for life."

"Sure, friends for life."

"I bet the others will be glad I have my own wagon."

Zander nodded. "Especially Dawn and Heath. Dawn often needs a place to by herself and the tent isn't set until late in the day. She and Heath are still trying to find their way."

"She's a very brave woman. What way are they trying to find?"

Zander turned a dark shade of crimson. "The married way."

She stared at him, waiting for more information.

"I'm not sure how to say this. Dawn would like a child, but she hasn't allowed Heath to—"

"You can stop right there. I know little about married folks."

"She usually sleeps in Cora's wagon. Though she spends time with Heath."

Tara sat down on a trunk. "I'm so uneducated. I should have known. I never know what to say to the women. I want to be friends with them but I don't know much about friendship. I do know that putting another in a position they don't want to be is not being a friend." Her heart sank. How did people make others like them? She never knew what to say, and she felt awkward.

"Could you guard my things for a few minutes? I want to talk to Harrison."

"Sure, but I doubt anyone will touch anything. If you're finished cleaning your wagon, I'll put your trunks and things inside."

"I wasn't looking for help. I'll be right back." Why did he always want to do things for her? Maybe because all his friends were married, and he saw them doing for their wives.

She found Dawn sitting in the wagon's shade reading. Tara took a deep breath; she needed to apologize.

"Mind if I sit with you?"

Dawn smiled at her. "Sure. It's nice and quiet here. It seems everyone is rummaging through the empty wagons."

Tara sat down. "I need to say something to you, and I'll let you know right off that I don't know how to be a friend. All I had was my Pa and once in a while some of his trapper friends. I know little about being a lady either. My ma died when I was seven, but she taught me what she could. What I'm trying to say is I'm sorry you and Heath aren't making children. I've been in your way and in your wagon. Forgive me?"

Dawn opened her mouth and then shut it again. She looked mad then she laughed. "Tara, you are a breath of fresh air. You know how to care for those around you. That's what makes you a good friend. I consider us friends, and I know Cora and Luella feel the same way. Sometimes it takes time to feel comfortable with someone. You just need to give the other person a chance." Her eyes widened. "Oh my, you might have given me a solution to my problem."

Tara smiled. "Glad to help. I need to talk to Harrison about some oxen." She stood and brushed the back of her pants to remove the dirt. "See ya later."

She found Harrison crouched by the rear wheel on his wagon. He smiled a greeting as he stood and faced her.

"I…have my wagon, what was mine and Pa's…and…"

"You need a yoke of oxen?" he asked as she wrestled with the words.

"Y-yes, sir, I do. I can pay a fair price."

He studied her for a piece, and she squared her shoulders, determined to pass muster. After a bit, he nodded. "I can help you. Let's talk terms while I show you my stock. It's been a rough go, but Zander, Heath, and Declan have done a fine job minding my animals.

Less than an hour later, they'd hammered out a deal for the oxen. Feeling on top of the world, she ran to her wagon to tell Zander. She found him standing by the oxen, checking the yoke and reins. A twig snapped beneath her foot, and he whirled, his expression the same that her father had worn before he exploded.

"Zander?"

"You're right, you are awkward. You go and tell Dawn what I told you? Heath was just here and he was mad because of my big mouth." He kicked at the ground, raising puffs of dust. "I'm glad I now know not to tell you anything. I feel like I've been hit in the head. I didn't see you as a carrier of tales. I thought you to be trustworthy." He stormed off, leaving her in his wake.

What just happened? Glancing around, she discovered everyone staring at her. Somehow she'd made one friend happy and another furious. Her stomach knotted, and she keenly felt the loss of Zander's friendship.

At a loss, she wandered over to the graves again and sat at her pa's marker.

"I'm not sure what to do, Pa. I must be a stupid fool, but I'm not sure why." Tears welled. "Oh, Pa, why did you have to leave me? I'm not prepared for life off the mountain. I thought I had made a dear friend, but he blew up at me. It hurts, Pa, his thoughts were important to me.

Silence settled around her except for the buzz of nearby insects. Her pa once would have offered sage advice... A sigh slipped out, and she swiped the backs of her hands over her eyes, drying the tears before they spilled over.

"Don't you worry none, Pa. I'll be just fine. You raised me to know how to take care of myself, and that's exactly what I will do. With the Lord's help I'll be in Oregon. I don't really know why we were going there. You aren't a farmer. I can only guess you wanted to raise cattle. Whatever I end up doing, I will make you proud of me. We'll be moving on in the morning, and I won't be back to visit, Pa. I will think about you every day. I know we never were ones for carin' words, but Pa, I love you." She looked up into the sky and then patted the earth where her father was buried.

She got up and rounded up the oxen Harrison had sold her. Then she yoked them. Once hitched to the wagon she was tempted mightily to go on her own, but that would be courtin' death. She drove the cattle near the wagon circle. There wasn't a space for her, but there would be. She took care of the oxen and then made a fire for herself. She could make flat bread and at the next stop she'd hunt.

While the bread baked, she filled her water barrel. She was not fond of the sulfur smell, but it didn't make anyone sick. Then she put the gifts she had taken for her friends in the flour sacks and then put the sacks into pots. The bread smelled heavenly as she took it off the fire. It would cool as she dropped off the packages.

With her arms full she walked toward the wagon she used to use. She couldn't wait for Cora, Luella and Dawn to see what she had. She never even got close. Zander saw her, stood and glared at her. He rattled her so that she hurried back to her own wagon. Her hands shook as she put the pots back into the wagon. Climbing in, she closed the tailgate behind her and cinched the canvas as tightly as possible. Her Bible was missing. It was odd, but perhaps other things would be noticed as time passed.

And it was fine. She knew most of the verses by heart.

CHAPTER FIVE

*A*s he stood guard duty, he couldn't help but watch Tara's wagon. He was still mad but Dawn had set him right. She had a good point. "We can never walk in another's shoes," she'd said. He'd spent enough time with Tara to know she didn't have a grasp of people. He should have made sure someone was sleeping under her wagon.

She ended up eating alone and had closed up her wagon very early. The strange thing was, Heath and Dawn smiled at each other and Heath touched her every chance he got. She was, in fact, still in the tent with him. Now he was the one who owed an apology.

The sadness and disbelief and confusion on her face haunted him all night. He'd be relieved soon, and then he'd sleep under Tara's wagon. He felt better just thinking about it. As soon as he was off duty, he grabbed his bedroll. He walked slowly and softly. He'd just situated his bedroll when someone sailed through the air and knocked him down.

He cursed under his breath. Why couldn't there have been a brighter moon? He fought back, surprised how strong the attacker was. Right before the knife plunged into him, he managed to roll them both so he was on top and straddling the miscreant. When he finally threw the knife and pinned the killer he took a breath and realized just how small the person was.

He saw the buckskins and groaned. "Tara?"

"Zander? Get off me! Get of me now! You are a low down snake—"

He put his hand over her mouth. "Shh. Someone is bound to come, and if they find us like this, it won't be good for either of us." He felt her relax and got off her.

She picked up the knife and grabbed his hand. Then she pushed him inside the wagon.

"What's going on?" Chuck Klass demanded.

"The ghosts are upset all their things were taken." She put her hands on her hips. "If needed, it was fine, but they're upset with those who took just for gain."

A strangled sound emerged from his throat. "Good night!" He ran back toward his wagon.

She climbed back into her wagon and put her hand over her mouth, stifling her laughter.

Zander did the same, then paused as a sliver of moonlight fell over her face. She was pretty when she laughed.

"I'm sorry I scared you, Tara. I thought someone should sleep under your wagon, and I felt awful about what I said to you. In fact, you made a difference in Dawn and Heath's relationship. If you could have seen the way they looked at each other and Heath touched her every chance he got and she didn't flinch." He sighed, wishing she would say something, anything. "No matter the outcome I should never have treated you that way and I am really sorry. You've been through a lot and you don't need me telling you what to do or chastising you."

She sat down and clasped her hands in her lap while she stared at them. "I didn't know I was doing anything wrong. I think my best bet is to keep to myself. I'll be just fine. I will see about buying a horse and paying someone to drive my wagon. It'll give me plenty of time to hunt for food. I thought I'd be fearful in this wagon since I'm not in the circle, but I'm not scared."

"You demonstrated that. You're tall but slim. Well not exactly slim, you have the right curves for a female. What I'm trying to say is you're surprisingly strong. I almost wasn't able to fight you off. I'm just glad we didn't get hurt."

She touched her cheek and glanced back down at her lap.

He lit the candle and groaned at the mark forming on her skin. "I did that? You're cheek is turning black and blue. I need to tend to the cut."

"It's my fault." She touched her face and winced. "My cheek landed on a rock when you got on top of me."

"Do you have a clean cloth I can use to tend to it?"

"What I think is that you'd best get out of my wagon. I'm surprised we haven't drawn a crowd." Her eyes held humor.

"Blast!" He hurried and blew out the candle. He reached the tailgate and turned back to her. "I'm sorry about yelling at you and about your cheek. Get some sleep." He jumped down before she answered him. After rolling onto his bedroll he wondered if she'd had to defend herself often in her life.

———

HE WOKE before her and snuck away. It was a cowardly move, but he didn't know what to say to her. He was sorry, but that was it. If she was looking for a man, it wouldn't be him. He started the fire outside the wagon they all used and made the coffee. He would have started breakfast, but apparently his cooking wasn't appreciated. Most of the food he used to steal was already made, so he'd never learned to cook.

Eli walked over and helped himself to a cup of coffee. "Got myself a new job and maybe a wife."

Zander cocked his brow. "Oh really?"

Eli smiled. "Many of the Culver cattle died and Mr. Culver doesn't want to pay me now. Only up to the time they died. That gal that wears trousers needs a driver, and I've been hired." He puffed out his chest. "It won't be long before she takes a likin' to me."

"I see. That happened quickly."

Eli turned red. "I was listening outside her wagon last night. I wanted to know if I could pay her for some services, if you know what I mean."

"You should be ashamed, listening to others. Besides, she's not like that."

Tilting his head, Eli directed a speculative, narrow-eyed glare at Zander. "Keeping her for yourself, are you? I heard you talk about her being on top and then you on top."

"What exactly are you planning?" Zander asked, keeping his voice even with an effort.

"I already struck a deal with her," Eli answered, a smug expression creeping over his face. "I doubt her services will be available anymore."

Zander started to his feet. Eli needed to learn a lesson.

"Good morning!" Tara practically sang out as she strode up, her fresh buckskins catching the morning light, making it appear she was glowing.

"I just told Zander about our deal," Eli announced with a sly smile. "I'll bring my things to the wagon. It'll be nice to sleep somewhere dry for a change."

Zander stared him down.

"I'll get my things now. I'll be back in plenty of time to get the oxen all hitched." Eli hummed as he left.

"You hired him awfully quick."

"Yes. I got lucky." Her smile widened. "He was waiting

outside the wagon hoping I had a job for him. I hired him right away."

"You do know what he meant about sleeping in a dry place, don't you?" he was forced to ask.

Tara's brow furrowed. "He'll be sleeping under the wagon instead of out in the open. Why, what do you think he meant?"

"I think he plans to sleep in the wagon with you."

She shook her head. "There isn't enough room for us to sleep separately… I think you have it all wrong, Zander. I need to get all packed up. Have a good day."

He shook his head as she walked away. How would she ever get along as naïve as she seemed most times?

"What's going on?" Heath asked in a pleasant tone.

Zander stared. His friend had a distinct look of happiness about him. "Perhaps I should ask you that very question."

"We… we're very happy together." Crimson swept up Heath's neck and flooded his face.

"Good." He smiled for his friend, but a sense of trouble stole some of his joy. "Tara hired Eli to drive her wagon. He thinks she is a prostitute and plans to sleep with her in the wagon."

"What? Did you warn her?"

He shook his head in frustration. "She is positive I'm wrong. Now I'll have to keep an eye on her," Zander complained.

Heath laughed. "You were watching out for her anyway. I don't understand the fallen woman thing. Is it because she wears those buckskins? That's just practical if you ask me."

"Not exactly." He frowned then went on to explain. "I thought I'd sleep under her wagon last night. She must have heard me and the next thing I knew she jumped from the back with a knife in her hand. It was dark, and I swore from her strength it was a man. We struggled until I got the upper hand. I guess we made enough noise for Chuck to nose around, and I jumped into the wagon so as not to be seen. When he left, I saw a cut on her cheek, and she said it happened when I rolled and got on top of her. Eli was snooping around her wagon and heard that and thought..." Heat crept into his cheeks.

Heath laughed so hard tears ran down his face. "How'd, How did she get rid of Chuck?"

A chuckle slipped out, and some warmth in his face eased. "She told him the ghosts from the wagons were unhappy because some people were greedy and took things they didn't need."

Heath clutched his stomach and kept laughing until he could hardly breathe. "He believed her?"

"He left, didn't he?" Zander was annoyed.

"That's the best laugh I've had in ages," Heath said, drawing a deep breath.

Harrison came to the fire and looked at both of them. "I just sold the bay mare to Tara. She'll pay extra when the foal comes or she'll give me the foal once it's weaned. She said she had a drover all lined up to take care of the animals."

Heath started to laugh. "She hired Eli."

"What's so funny?"

Heath gazed at Zander. "I'll tell you later. Right now Tara is convinced she made a good choice. We'd best keep our eyes open and sending up a few prayers to the Lord might not be a bad idea. I know he drinks and I'm not sure he knows one end of an ox from the other."

"Heath I need you to drive the wagon today and I want your wife off her feet. I saw her limping," Harrison said.

"We've tried and tried but her feet don't seem to want to heal completely. The Indians made her stand in hot coals. That, combined with the fact she didn't have shoes the whole time. I'll make sure she rests."

"The more I hear the more I wonder how she survived. Your wife is one brave and strong woman."

Heath smiled. "That she is."

———

TARA PATTED her new horse as they started to slow for the nooning. She'd gotten more than a fair deal from Harrison. The mare was excellently trained, but she didn't have a name. Well, she did. It was Bay Mare, The Pregnant One.

"I'll find something better for you pretty lady."

She was wondering if she had been too impetuous in hiring Eli. He wasn't the best of drivers, and once they reached the mountains again, she'd have to drive.

She tied the mare to the back of the wagon. Captain London wanted to talk to them. "There are trading posts as you can see. We'll be here for two hours and then onto where we split. One way will lead to California and the other to Oregon. Those of you going to California will need to pick a new Wagon Master. The who are going to California, gather at Tom Simps' wagon."

Tara headed back toward her wagon and came upon a few men talking and gesturing toward it. She didn't like the look in their eyes, not that she recognized them.

"Tara, come keep me company," Dawn yelled over to her.

Tara walked toward Dawn, but she kept her eyes on the men.

"Do you know them?" Dawn asked.

"No, I don't."

Dawn reached inside the wagon and drew out two rifles. She handed one to Tara. "They are interested in your wagon. Where is Eli?"

"His time is his own."

Dawn nodded but pressed her lips into a grim line.

"Why aren't you at the trading post?" Tara asked.

"I don't want to be near the Indians, and I'm not convinced that Kills Many has stopped looking for me. I'm anxious enough being here. I don't need to go."

"Kills Many?"

"The Lakota who kidnapped me and killed my baby. Another had the pleasure of killing my husband. I was with them for almost nine months." Dawn stared at her, waiting for something.

"My pa had dealings with all kinds of Indians. One stole my pa's pelts and tried to buy me with them. We were always armed, and we had a hidden tunnel out of the cabin as well as hidden supplies. I've seen all kinds. They're like whites—some are pleasant enough and some are snakes. Trappers are the same way. They knew not to mess with me because they were wary of my pa, and now my pa is gone, some might try. But I'll protect myself."

"Tara, we're alike in some ways. I always carry a knife. No one will ever take me again."

"You can count on me. I won't allow anyone to torture you again."

"Did Heath tell you what they did to me?" She looked troubled.

"No, I can see it in your eyes. I doubt many can see it if they haven't seen it before." She looked over her shoulder at the gathered group. "Those men are still talking about my wagon. I'm not sure I want to go back to it alone."

"We'll wait until the men get back. Zander will take you."

"True, but I hired Eli. I'll just wait for him." Needing a change of subject, she said, "I've heard the water will get stronger smelling from here. We should be at Fort Hall in about five days if we push it."

"We are alike in that way too. I always want to know

exactly where I am and where we are going so, I can find my way if I need to."

Tara smiled at Dawn. "Thank you for being my friend. Eli's heading this way. I'll see you this evening."

"Being your friend is easy," Dawn assured her. "Be careful!"

Tara walked toward her wagon and smiled at Eli. "Did you find anything useful at the trading posts?" she asked nodding toward the two burlap bags he had.

"Just a few things. They have readymade dresses if you want to get yourself one."

"I'm fine."

"I'm just suggesting it. The other women don't like you wearing men's clothes."

She studied Eli's face. "And that's important?"

"I would think so, if you plan to get yourself a husband, that is."

Tara shook her head. "I have no plans for such a thing."

"From what I've seen around here, you don't get a choice. The captain tells you when to marry. He don't cotton to any female traveling alone. Few men want a woman who wears pants for a wife."

She shrugged her shoulders. An odd sensation stole over her, and she had a feeling someone was watching her. When she looked around those same men were standing in the distance. She glanced at Eli but he didn't seem to notice the men. "Do you know those men over there?"

He glanced and shook his head. "Never seen 'em before. They probably rode ahead of their wagon train."

Ignoring the group of men as best she could, Tara climbed into the wagon and collected her gun belt. When she scrambled out of the wagon, Eli stared her up and down.

"That's not going to make you popular, you know. Men like women to be more feminine."

She scowled at him. "I don't want to hear your advice. I think we'll be pulling out soon. Go check on the oxen." Obviously, he'd be of no help as far as protection went.

As soon as Eli left two of the men, came her way. The rest of the group kept their distance, but when she risked a glance their way, they were watching. She took a deep breath and hovered her hand over her pistol.

Thanking God was the first thing she did when she felt Zander walk up behind her.

"Do you recognize any of these men?"

"No, but they've been watching the wagon the whole time. They make me nervous. What would they want with my wagon?"

He stepped closer behind her. "Maybe it's you they're watching. Where's Eli?"

"Getting the oxen." Zander didn't need to know her doubts about Eli.

The two men approaching differed greatly from one another. One looked more of a businessman with new clothes—fancy trousers and a white linen shirt. He even had a tie around his neck. The other man looked more like an outlaw, with his frayed trousers and stained red shirt. He kept a wide stance with his hand resting on his gun.

"Did you need something?" she asked warily.

"Yes, you can give me my wagon back," the outlaw said.

"And you are?" Zander asked.

"The name is Bennett. This wagon was part of a fleet of wagons I bought. It was being driven by a Patrick Carmichael to California for my boss, Mr. Cane."

"I take it you're Cane?" Zander asked the well-dressed man.

"Yes, and I would like my property back." His eyes narrowed as he looked between Zander and Tara.

"I've never seen you before," Tara said.

"It don't matter. This here wagon is going to California," Bennett said as he took a step forward.

There was no way she was giving up her wagon. She was about to tell them so, when Zander put himself between her and them. It wasn't the time to show annoyance. She'd let him know later how she didn't appreciate his high-handedness.

She heard a rifle being cocked behind her and then another and another. The next thing she knew she was shoved behind a crowd of men. She was tall but not tall enough to see what was happening.

Zander took her arm and dragged her to a wagon. A little roughly, he pushed her inside then sat in the front.

"What are you doing?" It outraged her.

"Saving your hide." He didn't turn around. "You know all that money you found? They know about it. That's why they want your wagon. I don't believe their story that it belongs to them. They didn't know where in the wagon the money would be. But you did. I'm getting you out of here and ahead of the rest for a bit."

The wagon lurched, and she fell to her knees as Zander drove off. Looking out the back she saw the line of people going to California blocking the way for anyone to follow them for a good while.

"How'd they get it all set up so quickly?"

"The captain had a feeling about them as soon as we stopped today. The California-bound wagons were ready to go but held off until I got you out of there."

Her eyes filled. They went to a lot of trouble to save her. Her father, must have been up to something, but it wouldn't have been anything shady. She knew that in her gut. He had talked about a great venture so he could rest his weary bones. He and his friends, he said. But they were going to Oregon, not California. Had he misled her? Was their destination California? He didn't seem to be the least worried.

"Are you all right back there?"

"Zander, will they take my wagon?"

"If you're worried about going broke, don't. You're among friends."

She smiled. He was a nice man. "I hid the money in your wagon. Not all of it. Some I have on me."

He quickly glanced over his shoulder. "You are smart. I don't think I would have taken any from the hiding spot." He looked straight ahead for a bit then glanced back again. "Unless I thought someone who already knew about the secret place was around."

"I did have a moment of doubt after hearing bits here and there about your life on the streets in Ireland. But I had a feeling someone would come gunning for me eventually, and I didn't want them to get their hands on the money."

He nodded but didn't say anything for a long while.

"Is it true no one will marry me because I wear pants?"

He laughed. "Where did you hear that?"

"Eli." Movement in the corner of her eye caught her attention, and she glanced over then gasped as a roiling gray-black mass loomed. "Look at the dust! It looks like a huge cloud coming at us!"

"Quick wet a cloth for me and then for the oxen. Cinch the back as tight as you can!"

She flew around the wagon, wetting cloths and handing them to him. The wagon dipped as he climbed down. She cinched the back, but it looked bad. Luckily, the storm was coming at the side of the wagon and not at the front. The wagon dipped again as Zander jumped onto the front and then into the back. He cinched the canvas as tightly as he could.

"Whew. I could hardly see the oxen out there. I put the

cloths around their heads covering their eyes. They are not happy."

She handed him another wet cloth and a cup of water.

"Thank you."

"How long do you think we'll be stuck here?"

"It could be hours. I really don't know."

Tara nodded. "You could tell me about your life in Ireland.

FOR A MOMENT, he didn't say a thing. So many memories came forward. "My parents died when I was young. First my father had an accident while shipbuilding. He lost his leg and there was no more money. My ma tried to find work, but her being so pretty there was only one job she was offered. I was around seven, and I brought food home. I'd snatch it here and there but soon we were evicted and were homeless. My pa grew horribly sick, so fast. The next thing we knew he was dead. My ma and I managed to get him buried at the church. I'd never been so thankful, Father Murphy allowed us to bury him on consecrated ground for no payment."

Tara remained silent.

Zander took a few minutes to gather his thoughts. "Then Ma and I went looking for a sister of my father's, but we never did find her. We slept in doorways when we could or alleyways. It was dangerous to be out after dark, and two men tried to grab my ma. She ended up dead from a stab wound. The authorities took me to an orphanage. It was not a place you'd ever want to be, but once in, it was near impossible to escape." He sighed. The less said about his time there, the better. Boys his age were sent to workhouses during the day and sheltered in the orphanage overnight. If any pay was to be had, he'd never seen it; the orphanage claimed it as due for his keep. "After a year, I had carved enough places in the stone wall surrounding the place for me to scale it halfway. I jumped and caught the top of the wall and dropped down the other side. I had to run as fast as I could. I hadn't counted on the other kids cheering and alerting the guards. It seemed like a long way back to Galway. Finally, when I was seventeen a captain hired me. I was always on the scrawny side and every year I'd try for a job, but no one would hire a lad who was likely to keel over with a bit of labor. I was might proud that day. We sailed to Boston, and I decided to stay. I met up with the Leary boys right away. We were competing for the same jobs on the dock. We pooled our resources and I had a home for the first time since I was seven."

"That's sad. You were on your own for a long time and so young." Her voice was so soft it warmed him.

"I learned to survive and not get caught. The last two years in Ireland people were starving in the street. Every morning there would be dead people all around. I had less to eat than normal, but I ate. They came to the cities thinking there would be work, but there wasn't any and there wasn't food or lodging for them either. I thanked God for a week straight when I got the job."

"Do you still speak to the Lord?"

"Not as much, I suppose," he admitted.

A gust of wind shook the wagon, and for a heartbeat, Zander feared they would be toppled, but it quickly calmed, though it still howled like an angry wolf.

"My father's Bible was missing from our wagon," she said, picking up the conversation again. "I know many of the verses, but sometimes just holding the holy book comforts me. I must find a new one, I suppose."

He chuckled. "You're in luck. The minister has a wagon full of them. He also holds ten-minute services on Sunday."

"I'd wondered what that was all about. It was so short I didn't think much about it."

"The captain waits for no one, not even God. Many thought we'd stop on Sundays and were upset when we didn't. I'd just as soon do what the Captain tells us. He's made many successful trips. I think he mentioned this was his last trip, and he was going home to his wife for good."

"She must be one understanding woman. He's gone more than he's home," she remarked.

"If they can make it work…" He shrugged.

"You never did answer me." She shifted in the cramped space and pinned him in her gaze. "Will no one ever marry me because I wear pants?"

"I don't know. Usually when a woman is trying to attract a man she wears something pretty. She acts all sweet and nice."

Sorrow briefly pinched her face. "That's the thing. I don't even know if I'm sweet and nice. I can cure your ailments and I could take down your enemy, but I don't think that's what you mean. I can dress a deer and make clothes from the skin. I can even light a pipe if needed. I've helped to build a barn, and I've patched the roof more times than I can count. I must admit I set a good trap too."

Zander smiled.

She smiled back. "A man wouldn't care about my skills, would he? He might not even like them. My pa often said I'd have a hard time finding someone to share my life with, but he also told me never to settle. He told me there was love out there, I just needed to find it. The problem is I don't know where to look." A scowl drew her eyebrows together. She certainly was expressive. "Eli keeps looking at me but it's not a loving look, it's more like he'd like to bed me look. My pa called it leering. It makes my skin crawl and I feel not quite clean."

KATHLEEN BALL

"It's best to keep your eye on Eli. He's been known to drink too much."

"You frown on drinking?"

Zander laughed. "I was raised on the stuff, but there's a difference between having a drink and being a drunk. You just be careful."

"I'm glad we're friends again. It feels nice to just sit here and not worry if I'm doing something wrong. I don't feel as though you're judging me. You just listen."

The wagon shuddered against the rising wind, this time tilting so far Zander knew a wheel had come off the ground. It shifted, and they were back on the ground. Her eyes opened wide. "Are we safe in here?"

"Truthfully there wasn't a place to take shelter, so this is it."

"What about trees? Maybe we could climb up high enough and get out of the dust."

"You climb trees too?"

"How do you think I hid from the men I borrowed the bedroll from? I climbed higher as they got closer."

An easy chuckle slipped past his lips. "You are a minx!"

The wagon almost tipped once more, and Zander pulled Tara onto the floor under him, tightening his arms around her as the wagon tilted again.

"I need to let the oxen go!"

"Don't go out there!"

"If I don't they'll die for sure." He didn't wait for a reply. He grabbed his wet cloth and climbed out the front. The wind was fierce, and he thought he'd end up going through the air. It was almost as hard to breathe as it was to see. He didn't wait to watch where the oxen went He jumped back onto the wagon and climbed in.

The canvas was flapping madly, and he was afraid it would rip. "Sit up in that corner while I redistribute the weight in here." He unstacked what he could and pushed what he could to the side the wind was coming at. He left a small spot for him and Tara, against the very back. Then he paused to grab the crock of water and drank right from it. He placed quilts down then had Tara lay on her side with her back to the tailgate while he eased himself between her and a trunk. If the wagon flipped, he hoped they'd land on top.

He pulled the last quilt over their heads and all and then waited until his eyes adjusted. Tara never once screamed or wailed; she just did what she was told to do. Her eyes were wide and he wrapped his arms around her holding her head to his shoulder.

His face and neck hurt as though tiny shards of glass had cut into him. The wind grew louder and the wagon teetered again and again.

"If we flip, roll away from the wagon as fast as you can," she told him, her voice somehow calm but urgent.

He smiled. She'd be a helpful wife to some man.

"Are you scared?" she asked, her breath against his neck.

"Yes, but having you here, helps. You're like a port in a storm." The wagon lifted and flipped, crashing down hard enough to splinter it. It took Zander a moment to realize with her arms around him, she had rolled them away from the wagon. He really hadn't thought it would work. The trunks lay in chaos, but they were all intact.

The wind kept blowing. Tara was wriggling under him and he realized that they lay on a big quilt. He helped her to wrap it over them and then use their body weight to keep it anchored. His heart was pumping. He'd been in many tight spots but that was the closest to death he'd ever been.

"I hope the others miss this weather," she yelled into his ear. She kept wiggling under him.

"I, um, Tara you need to stay still."

She was still for about a minute.

61

"Tara, if you don't stop, I can't be responsible."

"For what?"

"For this." He kissed her softly and gently and then he groaned, deepening the kiss. Her mouth was all he could think of. Her lips were soft, and she tasted like coffee. He never wanted to take his mouth from hers, but he knew better. He knew he had to find it within himself to stop.

He raised his head and shifted them both so only her head and top part of her body lay on him. He pushed her legs to the side of him all the while holding on to her. Something rumbled. Was that thunder? What kind of weather did America have?

"I've never been kissed before. It was nice," her voice was so full of doubt he felt bad for her.

"It was nice. It was very nice, and I wish I could keep kissing you, but it could lead to other things we're not ready for."

"You never want to marry, do you?"

"Not if I can help it. I've lost too many people already and I know I can keep myself warm and fed. Anyone else… I don't know if I could keep them alive. I just don't want to be responsible for anyone else." Strange how his voice didn't carry the usual conviction. Her kiss set him off balance.

"I'm not sure what my plans are now that my wagon is fire tinder. Well those men should leave me be now. It makes me feel a bit lost, but I'll be just fine. I know where I've been and how to get back if need be, and I also know how to get to Fort Hall. I will never allow myself to be lost again. I was thinking a soldier might take me for a wife. Surely he'd understand my need to carry weapons."

"Soldiers seem to like women they have rescued or are from the east so they can bring culture to the fort."

"You're teasing me, aren't you?"

He gave a slow shake of his head.

"Well, I have to decide before long. Once we're too far from the mountains, I won't see any trappers. I'm appreciated in their world. It's something I know. Or do I want to continue on and see what my father was up to? If you really think about it, we'll get to Oregon too late for planting. Cabins will have to go up quickly. I'll need to buy the tools needed, but I can get four walls and a fireplace set up before the first snow. I can hunt. I suppose I should worry about what I'll do when this storm ends. First things first, right?"

Had he let her down? Had she begun to hope that they would become a couple? The kiss was opposite of what he said. She didn't know about desire. He shouldn't have kissed her. His heart hurt when she moved a bit away from him. He never meant to hurt her. Where would she fit in? Her list of prospects will probably be short. She'd make a widower a nice wife, if he lived pretty far away from the nearest town. His mother had always tried to be a lady with dignity right to the last. She held her head up and pretended not to see the pity and disdain on others' faces. Tara was as far away from being a lady a person could get.

"The wind is starting to let up." He gazed down at her pale face.

"Yes, it'll be nice to have a bit of fresh air. I keep wondering what I've done wrong. Everything keeps getting taken from me. I'd like to visit with the minister sometime soon. Do you think God abandons people?"

"Never. I know it feels that way sometimes, but that's the wonder of faith. He's always with us, and we never walk alone. I had to keep that knowledge in my heart after my folks died. I think I might have just crumpled and died if I didn't have faith." Though he'd been a little distant from God lately, he admitted to himself.

"It's hard." Her voice was full of unshed tears.

"I know it is, honey. I know."

KATHLEEN BALL

The pounding of horse hooves startled them. They quickly got up and both pulled a pistol. Zander was relieved it was people from the wagon train. There wasn't a place to hide. He smiled when he saw Heath and Declan. They had become his family.

He somehow got separated from Tara, but he caught a glimpse of her talking to Reverend Paul. She clung to her new Bible and turned away, walked away from the circle and stood alone looking out at the view. Zander didn't know if she felt alone or not, but he felt it for her.

LATER, she stood near her trunks. All had survived, though most required being dug out of the sand covering them. But their survival didn't solve her problem. How would she get her things to Fort Hall? She'd have to leave much of it behind. But she was alive and so was Zander. Her belongings didn't really matter in the long run.

"I guess it's up to me to give her shelter," a man said. She didn't recognize the voice and wasn't in the mood for a confrontation.

"Why would you give her shelter?" a second male asked.

"I'd teach her how to mind a man. She'd be wearing skirts or she wouldn't be able to sit down without pain. I didn't mention marriage. I'm saving myself for a proper wife."

She started to seethe.

"I'd marry her, myself. This way the law couldn't do a thing when I beat her into submission. I bet she's been with plenty of those mountain men. That's what they do — they have one female and share her."

"Chuck, you made that up. They wouldn't bother to share they'd just steal themselves a woman."

64

Well, at least she now knew one of the men. Chuck Klass, who had run away from her wagon, afraid of ghosts.

"Well, someone has to take her. Women can't travel alone. I thought a marriage between her and Eli was understood, but he says no, we're welcome to her." The man snorted. "I have to warn you, Eddie, she carries a gun."

"That's just not right. She's a female," Eddie said.

"Tell *her* that! She doesn't seem to know it except probably under the covers," Chuck said.

She whirled on them and drew her gun. "Take your crass talk and get out of my sight." She waited until they were gone before she stepped away from her trunks and let herself be sick. Now she knew what people thought of her. Some morals in the mountains weren't the same as down here, but she'd saved herself for marriage. Every man up there knew not to tangle with her.

No one had stepped up and offered to help her. It had been a long tense day, and a lot of it was due to her. People were probably sick of her.

After sweeping the sand away, she opened her trunks and rearranged the items. She lifted one and carried it to Dawn and Luella's wagon. No one was around so she left the presents she had collected for them on the ground. She took Cora's out and carried the pot down to her wagon. No one was there either.

Glancing around, she saw many people gathered around the livestock. She walked over to see what was happening. Chuck and Eddie were pushing each other back and forth while yelling out their claim to her. Eddie fell to the ground, and Chuck held his hands up in victory.

"That little hellion is mine!"

She took a step forward. "I'd rather be left behind." She turned and glared at the people in the crowd and almost gasped when she saw the captain plus all the people she had called friend. "No one asked me about this! I have no rights? To think I was looking forward to going to Oregon. Not anymore. I'm done with all of you!" She turned on one foot and ran to her trunks. She filled a couple burlap bags full of supplies. Then she went in search of her mare. Poor baby, she did need a name. She vaulted onto the horse's back and rode toward Fort Hall. She'd be able to hide well enough in case those men came back. She'd have to find a way to get her money back, but that was the least of her problems. And she trusted Zander. Thankfully, it would be dark soon; she'd need to find a place to hide.

CHAPTER SIX

*I*t had been two days since he'd seen Tara. At first he didn't realize she'd taken her mare. By that time, it was dark. He'd found her trail a few times, but it disappeared every time. This morning he was standing with the others at a grave. People said it had been a snake bite. Why didn't people just ask for help? Was it easier to die than to ask a favor?

Dawn was busy cleaning the wagon out; she'd claimed it for Tara. She and the other wives were determined to find her and bring her to Oregon with them. He'd seen their speculative looks. He was as worried about her as anyone but she would not be his wife because he felt sorry for her. Marriage was for life. He'd get over any pity he felt soon enough and he'd be left with a woman who didn't know how to be a woman.

She was a quick learner; he supposed. Her cooking was better than passable and she looked pretty when she smiled, but that did not mean she'd be a good wife. He was young still and he wanted to take his time looking.

They were ready to ride out. Eli was driving Tara's new

wagon, and they would be to Fort Hall the next day. Was she already there? Was she being treated with respect? Zander'd love to strangle both Chuck and Eddie. Where had they gotten the ridiculous idea that they could marry Tara?

Just thinking her name made his heart beat a little faster. He missed her. They had become good friends, and he'd thought them to be closer than ever after the storm, but she had so easily rode away without a word to him. If he was in the admitting mood, he'd might say he was a tiny bit hurt.

THERE HAD BEEN a bevy of shady characters riding in and out of Fort Hall most of the day. The wagon party was taking its sweet time getting there. Maybe she should go back and make sure they were all right. Her stomach knotted. No one had come looking for her. She'd thought, hoped… It didn't matter. There were many things that weren't meant to be. She opened her bible and leaned back against a tree and read. Waiting a while longer was probably a good choice.

The day went on, growing later and later. Tara stood, stretched, put her Bible in one bag she'd tied to her mare and then led the mare out of the tree line. She'd go on in., she could protect herself. The fort was white adobe and smaller than she'd imagined. There were several teepees set up and a lot of trading going on. She felt the stares of the Indians and the trappers as she walked by. She also saw the cold shoulder type of looks people from another wagon train gave her. She entered the fort and tied the mare to a hitching post before she walked into the store. She wanted to laugh when she saw the prices. They were double those of the store at Fort Bridger, and more than three times the prices she and her Pa had paid at trading posts near her home, and she had a feeling those had been on the high side to begin with.

Looking around, she noticed some dresses. None were new, but they were in good shape. Maybe Zander was right, maybe she needed to dress like a woman. She could live by herself but did she want to? Maybe she'd have to meet a few fellas to know. She picked out three that looked clean and next to new. Then she added a few hairpins and a bonnet. Finally, she had the proprietor put cheese and bread in with her order.

"You do have real money, don't you?" the tall man asked. With his hair greased back, he should have been stylish, but instead, he looked like he needed a bath. He gave her the shivers.

"Yes, I have a bit left," she admitted.

The man nodded and cut a big wedge of cheese and picked out bread for her. He wrapped it all up, and she acted as though she'd just paid her last cent—which wasn't hard to do, since the money she carried was nearly gone, and there were no guarantees she would get to that which she had stashed with Zander. She walked out onto the board walk and bumped into a bear of a man. Glancing at his face, she recognized him and smiled.

"Well, I'll be! Big Red, what are you doing in these parts?"

He took her packages and set them on a bench. Then he picked her up by the waist and swung her around. "Tara, my love! It's good to see you! Where's your pa? He promised me a ride to Oregon if I made it this far."

Her smile faded when he set her down. "Big Red, Pa and all them are dead."

LATER, as she bathed and put on one of her new dresses, a tear trailed down her face. Quickly she brushed it away. Big Red was taking her to supper in the soldiers' dining room. To think she was the one who had to comfort the big man. Her father had been going to Oregon after all. Her Pa had told Big Red that he'd bought a business and they'd all be rich and able to live in style. Big Red hadn't asked any details; he'd just jumped on the idea of having people around for a change.

She checked her hair in the room's mirror she had rented for the night. It would have to do. The dresses were long, but she could fix them by morning. The dark blue one she wore was serviceable. She hadn't looked for pretty dresses just useful ones. She'd had two dresses when she'd started the trip. Her pa thought it better that the men respected her as a woman. She had only worn them to please her pa.

Drawing a deep breath, she let it out slowly and stepped through the door into the hallway beyond. She walked down the stairs, and Big Red was there waiting for her. He was unusually tall and muscular, and his hair, which was the color of a carrot, hung well below his shoulders with curls going every direction. He'd been known to be fierce in a fight but not quick to anger. Her pa had said younger men always challenged him to fight, and Big would try to get out of it. Oftentimes he did, but once in a while he'd end up proving he shouldn't be tangled with. She'd known him forever, and he'd always brought her carved animals when he visited.

"Well look at you. You've turned into a fine young woman. I bet your pa was pleased with you. You can still skin a rabbit, can't you?" His laugh boomed in the confined space.

"Of course I can." She put her hand round his arm and into the crook of his elbow, allowing him to escort her into the dining hall. She startled when she heard the chairs all scraping the floor at once and then all the men standing.

Many nodded and called her ma'am. They sat back down after Big seated her.

"Looks like you've caught the eye of every buck here. We'll need to use our fancy manners tonight."

Her face heated as she laughed. "It's a good thing we practiced a time or two then."

They talked about days gone by and what would happen now. Big Red still planned to go to Oregon. "I'll look for a wagon for us in the morning. A few groups have been through here and many more are expected. We can join up with one."

"They won't let us."

He frowned. "Why not?"

"We're not related or married, so we can't travel together."

He winked at her. "Would you rather be my niece or my wife?"

"If you were twenty years younger—"

"My niece it is. Your Ma's brother since we have different last names."

They drank coffee after their meal, and then he walked her out into the moonlight.

He held her hand as they walked. "I still find it hard to believe that your pa and a lot of our friends were killed. Most of those men could have wrestled a bear and won. You found nothing strange in the wagon when it broke to pieces?"

If only she could trust him, she'd tell him about the money. "No."

"Your pa said Oregon. He wouldn't have had me meet him here if he had any plans to go to California. Those men were trying to trick you into something. We'd best be on the lookout for them as we travel." He walked her to the stairs leading to her room. Before he left, he bent and gave her a kiss on the cheek. "I'll see you bright and early, my girl."

Things would work out after all.

"I think you enjoyed that man's kiss better than mine."

She quickly turned and there stood Zander. Her heart beat so fast and loud she was sure he could hear it.

"When did you get here?" She smiled and stared at him. She hadn't been sure she'd see him again.

She took a step toward him, and he took one back. Stiffening, she frowned. "You don't seem to be as happy to see me."

"I see wearing a dress worked. I could also see from his expression that man loves you. Congratulations on your quick conquest."

"Why are you acting this way?" She tilted her head and studied his face, searching for… she didn't know what. But it didn't matter since all she found was an expression hard as flint. "I foolishly thought you might be happy to see me. I never know where I stand with you. Maybe you don't realize it, but you've toyed with me. One minute you say you will never marry and then the next you kiss me. Well now the idea of friendship doesn't appeal to me at all. I'll be joining a wagon party soon. Best of luck to you and may God keep you safe."

She turned and walked up the stairs. She walked slowly, though, hoping he'd call her back. But by the time she reached the top, tears streamed down her face. Once in her room, she clutched the pillow to her and cried out her pain. What might have been minutes or hours passed, and exhaustion hit her, so she changed for bed.

Thank you, Lord, for putting Big Red in my path.

Her eyes closed.

THE NEXT MORNING she dressed and packed her things. If Big Red said he'd find a wagon, then he would. She was eager to keep moving. She never wanted to see the murderers again. Somehow she knew they'd turn up at some point. It was like being with family again and it had been a long while since she hadn't felt of dread when she woke. She walked down the stairs and there was Big Red holding her mare's reins.

"Good morning." She smiled. "Does this mean we're getting ready to go?"

"The wagon is all stocked and ready, and the captain is real nice. The people too. One group asked me to bring you by for breakfast."

"That sounds wonderful!" She walked beside him out of the Fort and as soon as they approached the circle of wagons she knew what party they were.

"You said you have a wagon here?"

"Yes and this is the group you traveled with. You'll know people."

She nodded and tried to look happy. Maybe there'd been a reason she'd left them. But Big Red looked so proud of himself, she stayed quiet.

Cora ran to her and hugged her along with Luella and Dawn.

"We were thinking we'd never see you again," Cora said.

"Welcome back!" Luella said.

"I knew you'd travel with us again," said Dawn.

"Cora, Dawn, Luella this is, Big Red, my uncle." When she said *uncle*, Zander loudly said *husband* at the same time. Tara gave Zander a glare and walked to the fire. Just who did he think he was?

Zander stepped close to her. "Uncle?"

"He certainly isn't my husband," she growled as she put her hands on her hips.

"Say, I'm glad you brought her back to us Big Red," Captain London interrupted. "Tara did you see your wagon? Dawn cleaned it all up and then her husband and friends loaded it with your things. Big Red here stocked it with food and supplies. You certainly do have a generous *uncle.*" He stared at Zander until he backed up a bit.

"Thank you, Captain. Thank you everyone. I didn't think you'd want me back since those men are following me. But I have to admit I had hoped. I missed you." She made sure not to glance at Zander once.

She took Big Red's hand and pulled him along while she followed the other women. The wagon looked new and it was slightly bigger than the one she had. Tears filled her eyes as she peered inside. She gasped as Big Red lifted her into it. She'd have to remember she had someone to help her. She was indeed going to Oregon!

———

ZANDER FREQUENTLY FOUND his gaze wandering toward Tara and Big Red. She treated the burly trapper as more than just an uncle. They enjoyed each other's company a little too much, if anyone asked him. Tara had fired Eli and now Big Red drove and took care of the animals. He slept under the wagon, but Zander could see they were close. She was even back to wearing dresses. She didn't fool him.

They'd been traveling a week, and the Captain announced they'd have a later start the next morning. Everyone was excited. There would be music and dancing and hopefully whiskey. He could use a drink to unwind. He felt as though all he did was watch Tara and her uncle. She'd glared at him often enough.

He wanted to see how close she and Big Red danced together. Why it mattered so much to him he wasn't sure, but it did. He needed to look around at the other unmarried women. It wasn't good for him to be fixated on just one who loved another.

He did believe that they had known each other before and that he knew her father. But all this hand holding and calling her his girl was a bit much.

Zander couldn't stop remembering the kiss they shared, and he'd thought it meant something to her. No, he *knew* it meant something to her, but she'd played him for a fool. The only person he could trust was himself. It was a lonely feeling. He still had Declan, Heath, and Harrison, but somehow he felt alone. He longed for someone who wanted to listen to his dreams, to listen to his thoughts and tell him his fears and ideas weren't stupid.

He hadn't known he missed these things until everyone around him had started to get married. Harrison was busy with Cora and Essie. Declan had Luella, who had been sick, and Heath had begun to disappear with Dawn at all hours.

That left just him.

"I DON'T THINK I'm going to go," Tara told Big Red as her shoulders slumped. Being rejected day after day had finally gotten to her. Why bother to be cheerful? It wouldn't matter if she went or not.

"Who am I supposed to scurry around the dancefloor? Most of the women here seem to be afraid of me." He grinned as though it was a good thing.

"So, you've been watching the other women, have you?" she teased.

"I sure have. This old trapper has been alone too long. Some of these men aren't even kind and their woman still cooks for them. In fact, women have a lot to do all day long. I wouldn't mind a little tenderness in my life for a change."

She threw a piece of wood onto the fire. "Did you ever get married?"

"Almost..." His smile turned sad. "She was a beautiful girl, and we were friends. We snuck a few kisses, and we were to be married, but her father had other ideas. My family had a big spread in Texas, but he'd found someone with even more property. Her loyalty was to her father. She just shrugged when I confronted her. That's the day I left Texas and ended up trapping. I'd heard tell of beautiful lush lands in the Smokey Mountains from a man who once worked for me. So I went there and built my whole life in those mountains, and it was a solitary life, but it suited. Your pa was one of the few friends I had up there." A heavy sigh burst from him, and he shook his head. "I regret not looking for another to love. But that's why we're going to Oregon, to start new lives." He looked so serious.

"Let me just change my dress, and we can get going." The smile he gave her was worth her sacrifice.

She had one dress she hadn't worn yet. It was serviceable and yellow. Why she had thought yellow would be a good choice, she didn't know. It would show the slightest bit of dirt too quickly. She started to put her hair up but thought better of it. It really didn't matter what she did; some still acted like she had a gun drawn on them. Little did they know she had sewn pockets in her dresses for her pistol and a small one at her waist for her knife.

No one had commented on her dresses thus far, and maybe that was for the best. She had really wanted to wear her buckskins but hadn't wanted to cause another stir. But it was downright miserable trying to track a deer in a dress. Searching for signs they were being followed wasn't made any easier with a dress on either.

She'd dance with Big Red only. There really was only one other she wanted to dance with, but he'd been courting Leona Felton. She was nice enough, but Tara only felt jealousy when she glanced at her. Zander smiled at Leona and she had watched them walking one night. She'd quickly said a rushed goodnight to Big and retreated into the wagon to sulk. There wasn't anything she could do about it, but it wasn't easy.

Big Red helped her down from the wagon and offered her his arm. After taking a fortifying breath she went with him to the dancing. The music made her smile. The lively strains of a fiddle, guitar, and harmonica were particularly uplifting.

Big Red took her hand and swung her into his arms. She'd learned to dance while standing on his feet. That was so long ago. And now, they danced well together as though they could read each other's thoughts before every move was made. Staring into his eyes, she smiled. "We're still good dancers. I think people are staring at us."

He winked at her. "Let them stare. I bet they never thought of either of us as being light on our feet. It reminds me of when you were just a girl with braids who stuck to me like a burr every time I visited. Those were good times. You and your pa were my only family as far as I was concerned. Remember the time you decided that you wanted to wear a union suit to bed like me and your pa?" He laughed loudly for a moment and then grew serious. "Your mother would be so proud of how lovely you are. You look so much like her. Your pa was a lucky man."

"My face is turning red, isn't it?"

""
.

They danced most of the night together, neither one caring about the crowd of people all around them. She wished she could have said she never took her eyes off her friend but she knew where Zander was every moment. And her heart hurt as he danced with Leona and then sat with her talking.

"I can't watch anymore," Big Red said. "You wear your heart on your sleeve. It makes me want to have a chat with Zander."

"No, he didn't do anything. I suppose it was just girlish

dreams. He… he can make his choice, and he did. Just promise we won't settle down near him. I don't think I could take seeing him married with babies—" Her voice broke as a swell of emotions rippled through her, thinking of Zander and babies.

Big Red stopped dancing and put his arm around her. "Let's get you back to the wagon. I'm sorry I made you come, but I enjoyed myself immensely."

"Dancing was fun. I'm ready to go, though." They walked away from the other dancers. Before they got very far, Mandy Echols another single woman smiled at Big Red. Tara felt him hesitate, and she stopped. "I'll meet up with you later." She stood on her toes and kissed his cheek before she turned and walked back to the wagon alone.

He deserved to be happy, though she didn't know a thing about Mandy. A place in her heart smiled for him even as the rest of her heart wanted to weep. Big Red was a handsome man; he could have his choice of women, Zander could too. She didn't have the right to think badly of Zander. Maybe badly was the wrong word. She was hurt and that was about it. She put the coffee on to heat and then sat by the fire.

It's been quite the journey, Lord. I feel as though I've lived many lifetimes in the past few months and perhaps I have. I've grown from a naïve girl to a woman who has so many feelings. New feelings; some good and some bad. I grew up exposed to the miracles of nature but I didn't know and still don't know how to act or be with these people. I don't belong somehow. Thank you for bringing Big Red to me. I can trust him, and there is a lot to be said for trust. I feel like a fraud all fancied up in this dress and acting like a lady. I'm just me. I'm good at being just me. Anything else just seems like a big lie. I am strong Lord. You made me this way, and I will find my way. Bless us all as we travel. Thank you, God.

She poured her coffee and sipped it, listening to the music. A few young men walked by with a jug of whiskey.

They nudged each other, but they didn't say a word. It was time to turn in. She took the coffee out of the hot coals and banked the fire. Upon straightening up she saw Zander walking Leona Felton to her family's wagon. Holding her breath, she waited for him to kiss her and from Leona's expression, she waited too.

But Zander didn't kiss her. How odd.

She stepped up and into the wagon, and before she could cinch, the canvas closed Zander was there staring at her face.

"Hello," he said softly.

"Hello," she echoed back.

"You look like an angel when you dance." The words almost seemed torn from him, and his normal lilting accent had thickened. "You're so graceful, I guess it surprised me. You and Big Red look as though you've danced together for years."

Shyness washed over her, but she held his gaze. "We have. I learned to dance by standing on his boots as he danced me across the cabin floor. He was one of my pa's best friends, and he always gave me a wooden animal he'd carved. I might not be his niece by blood, but he is family. I love him as an uncle." She made a helpless gesture in the air with her hands. "It was a bit of a miracle he was at the Fort, or I'm thinking it was God's handiwork with a bit of inspiration from my pa. You see, I doubt I would have been able to join this party again unless I was married, and I'm sorry, but the only man I know interested—perhaps—was Eli. I would have passed on it and waited for another wagon train group to stop at the Fort. I was nervous about those men riding up to Fort Hall. I stayed in the woods for two days before I was brave enough to go inside."

"I missed you."

"How much whiskey have you had?" She laughed.

He scowled. "I pared it down to only one swig. So, it's not the drink talking, it's me."

"You and Leona make a good couple." She held her breath. What if he agreed? *Please don't agree with me.*

"She's nice enough, maybe a bit too nice."

"She doesn't try to knife you?" Some of her tension eased. "I'm disappointed."

He studied her face, and she wondered what he saw.

"Big Red is on his way. Good night, Zander."

"Good night, Tara-mine."

He was gone before she could ask him what he meant. His visit had been a balm to her heart. She wouldn't have to watch him with Leona for the rest of the journey.

Big Red shook his head at her. "You should see the joy on your face. You have it bad for Zander. I'm glad you two are talking. Good night." He grabbed his bedroll and was gone.

Thank you, Lord.

CHAPTER SEVEN

$\mathcal{I}$t was hard going, watching the Snake River flow down in the canyon while they were several hundred feet above it and unable to reach what they could see and hear. They'd been warned to conserve water and as they traveled through the sparsest land Zander had ever seen, he prayed better things were coming in the next few days. The cattle were feeling it, and they were slowing. It was so very hot, so they simply couldn't hurry through the area without losing the livestock.

They'd finally come to a spot where they could possibly lead the animals to the river, though it was still steep. They felt they needed to take the chance. It was, as with most of the trip, the animals that had been well treated and cared for had difficulty, but they were able to get back up the steep climb after they drank their fill. The livestock that were more like walking bones weren't able to make it back up.

They'd managed to get all of Harrison's stock back on the trail. It was slow going, and he, Declan, and Heath had needed to push some upwards. Harrison and Big Red lassoed many and helped them up. They were also able to fill their water barrels through sheer strength. Big Red made extra trips for the widow ladies and some older travelers.

There was much grumbling when the other drovers weren't helping or exerting any extra energy. They just left the oxen in the canyon, uncaring of their fate.

Zander realized he and Big Red were like-minded in wanting to make some of the drovers go back down into the canyon, but it wasn't their business or so they were told. They both planned to get up early and see if, after a night of rest, they could encourage any more to come back up.

What did folks intend to do? Walk? They needed their livestock to pull their wagons. He didn't understand why more people weren't outraged.

"They're tired," Tara explained as she fed them both. "Some of those drovers are bullies. The livestock owners are upset, but they don't know what to do. I heard a few mentioning putting bullets in the drovers."

"The captain will figure things out, I suppose," Zander said. "This is good. Where d'you get the salmon?"

Her eyes widened and she looked as though she'd been caught doing something she shouldn't have.

"You might as well tell him," Big Red suggested.

"I just did a bit of fishing is all."

"I didn't see any woman at the river."

"I wore my buckskins and put my hair up into a hat. No one bothered me, and I was able to feed a whole lot of people."

He sat still, stunned that he hadn't noticed her. Thinking back there was a little fella going up and down the hill with a basket. Glancing around, he saw many people eating salmon.

"You caught enough fish to feed everyone?"

"No, not all the drovers have fish to eat."

Zander started to laugh. "Leave it to you to get the point across in the best way possible."

"You sure helped to put a few fires out, young lady," Captain London said as he helped himself to a tin cup and filled it with coffee. "We'll give people a bit of time in the morning to get the oxen back up. If not they must make other arrangements. I warned them." He drank down the coffee, nodded his thanks and moved along.

"Tara! Do you think you can watch Essie? Everyone seems to have disappeared," Cora held the wiggly baby girl out to her. "I can figure where Dawn and Heath are, but I'm worried about Luella. Her bout of morning sickness is much worse than I've ever seen, and I'd like to spend some time pampering her, if a person can be pampered in this desert heat. I'll send Declan out to take a breath. He looks so worried."

Cora handed Essie to Tara and headed for Luella's tent.

Tara's eyes widened as she examined the baby. "What am I supposed to do with this? Last time she cried and Zander took her."

Big Red laughed. "I imagine the same thing you did with that baby bobcat you brought home."

Instantly, she had Essie in her arms and was rocking her. "She's bigger than Bob was but almost as cute."

"You had a baby bobcat?" Zander stared at her.

"I found her alone and crying. Of course I brought her home. I even knitted her a blanket. My Pa wasn't a big fan of Bob."

"You called a female Bob?"

"It made the most sense. I only had her for about five months. She started eating up everything in the cabin including a table. She stayed close to the cabin for a while but one day she never came back. I was upset, but she probably found a family of her own." She placed a kiss on the baby's cheek. She looked good with a baby in her arms.

Zander forced himself to glance away. Those were not

observations he wanted to make. Besides, she had Big Red, and she didn't need him any longer.

Declan joined them looking a bit down. "We will only have the one child. I'm not putting Luella through this again. She's sick all day."

Harrison chuckled, taking a seat. "Most women get morning sickness or in Luella's case all day sickness but it only lasts for a while."

"How long is a while?" Declan asked with a hopeful look in his eyes.

"I think a couple months. This is Cora and my first pregnancy together. She told me women are all different, and Luella's being sick is uncomfortable and sometimes it might seem horrid but it's normal."

"Horrid is a good word for it." Declan agreed.

"I think once you hold the child all the hard times will be forgotten," Harrison said.

Essie started cooing and everyone smiled. Zander had a hard time glancing away from Tara again. "I have guard duty. Night all." He couldn't help himself he found himself gazing at Tara and Essie again and he felt as though he'd been kicked in the stomach. It's what he wanted.

He finally walked way. What was wrong with him? She was not for him. In fact, he didn't want a wife. If only he could remember that when she was near.

WHAT A MORNING! Tara and the other women packed up and got the livestock hitched while their men were down in the canyon trying to get the rest of the animals up the hill. One by one she saw oxen make it up to the top, but not as many as she had hoped. People argued, and words got heated as to whose fault it was. Tara waited by the wagon with her gun in her pocket. Big Red headed over. "Honey, throw me out a fresh pair of buckskins." He was covered in mud. Even his hair was matted.

"Where do you plan to change?"

"Out here, I'll keep my back to the others and if they want to peek at what the good Lord gave me, then that's up to them." He grinned at her.

Tara grabbed him some clean clothes. "I wish we could spare the water to wash you. How far did you fall? Are you hurt?"

"I didn't fall, wait until you see your Zander." Big Red laughed as he unlaced his buckskins.

Face flaming, Tara turned her back while he changed.

"I'll hang the muddy ones on the side of the wagon. They'll dry and then we can brush them out."

"It's *we* who will get the mud off *your* clothes?" She enjoyed her merry banter with Big Red until she saw Leona stop Zander and take his hand.

Tara watched as Leona used her hand to wash Zander and then urged him to take off his shirt. The woman even washed his hair for him!

She couldn't pretend she didn't care, so she took cover in the wagon, tears stinging her eyes. Leona was pretty, and she had flattering clothes on. It was said she was a good cook and that she had gone to a good school back East. She wasn't practical, though, using an entire bucket of water to wash Zander. He should have stopped her for the sake of saving water. After quickly brushing away an errant tear, Tara jumped out of the wagon and began to walk in the direction they were going. She'd walk. All the animals needed special handling, including her mare. She had no idea when they'd see fresh water again.

She walked fast enough that she could walk alone. She didn't feel like talking to anyone. Keeping up aimless chatter with the women would have been too hard. After a few hours, she slowed until she was with her group of friends. Luella looked peaked, and Tara had Big Red pull off. Then she crawled inside and took a trunk out of the wagon.

She and Big Red shared a look and the man picked Luella up and placed her inside the wagon along with a crock of water. Luella was at first upset until she realized what was going on. "Thank you," she said tearfully.

"Just rest and don't let Big Red talk too much."

Chuckling, Big Red kissed Tara's cheek before he climbed back on the wagon and started out again.

"That was the sweetest thing I've ever seen," Dawn said as Cora nodded in agreement.

"Not so sweet, it was all Big Red's stuff in the trunk."

"Really?" The women laughed.

"No not all, but we can easily make ourselves more clothes and things. Living in the mountains we make do with what we have and we have been abundantly blessed."

Declan caught up to the women. "Where's Luella?"

"She's in Tara's wagon. Tara threw out a trunk so Luella wouldn't be added weight," Cora yelled up to him.

He nodded as he had the lines loose in his hands. "This wagon had accumulated a lot of things. We'll need to go through it tonight. Tara that was very thoughtful of you, and I thank you from the bottom of my heart."

Her face heated. "It's just things. Luella is worth much more, and you are welcome."

Declan drove past them and next was Leona riding beside her father in the wagon. Was the girl ill or hurt? Leona turned her head away when she came even with them. After they pulled forward, Cora shook her head.

A need to know what happened had Tara asking if Leona was hurt.

"No, just selfish, I guess," Dawn said.

"She's never walked," Cora added, shaking her head.

It was a wonder why Zander spent time with Leona. Perhaps he appreciated her beauty. It must be something.

Tara's chin wobbled until she clamped her jaw tight. It was no use. The more she tried not to think about that man, the more he was on her mind. Tara watched a few wagons drive by with cattle pulling them. It was the strangest sight.

"We need grass and water soon."

"We sure do," said Dawn. "It looks like we will stop for the nooning."

There wasn't room for a circle and everyone just stopped where they were. Zander caught up to them on one of Harrison's horses. "The captain said it'll be a quick stop. If we keep going, we'll make it to a creek by nightfall. He also said to be sure to water your livestock." He lingered for a bit.

"You're welcome to come eat at my wagon," Tara said as she gazed at him. Then she looked at Cora and Dawn. "I still have plenty of fish. I cooked it all last night. If we're going to be at a creek, there'll be game there."

"I'll meet you there." He urged the horse forward

"Zander?" Tara called after him.

He looked over his shoulder but didn't stop his mount. "Yes?"

"Could you tell Harrison, Declan, and Heath to join us?"

He smiled at her. "I sure can."

She was still feeling warm from his gaze as the continued on to her wagon.

"I feel something akin to love in the air when you and Zander are together," Dawn teased.

"Maybe at one point, but he's made it very clear that he doesn't want a wife. I can't allow my heart to go down that road with him again."

Cora nodded. "I can understand that."

When they arrived at the wagon, Tara quickly served

them. They were hesitant to use any of their water but Tara convinced them they had plenty. It was a hot dusty meal with mosquitoes still swarming but she felt as though they were family. She still wouldn't be able to live near Zander and see him marry another, but for now it was a nice feeling.

ZANDER STAYED after the rest left Tara's wagon. Few women would part with their things so another could ride. She impressed him.

"Do you see how the road narrows up ahead?" Zander asked Tara. "Keep your eyes on the rocks above. I've seen a few shadows up there, and it would be a good place for an ambush. Have your rifles loaded and ready," he instructed. "Tara, ride in the wagon ready to shoot out the back. I already talked to the others and Captain London and Oscar are telling the rest of the party."

"It's the men after me, isn't it?" Tara sounded weary.

"Maybe," he hedged. "I don't know."

"Well I do know, and I'm driving the wagon, and I'm going first!"

Big Red stood and stared at Tara. "Not without me, you don't. I'll be driving. It's them, I can feel it. I knew someone was watching us today, but I missed the shadows. Thanks for letting us know, Zander."

Tara got busy putting everything away and getting the rifles ready. "Be careful, Zander."

"Are you really planning on taking the lead?"

"It's only right." She jumped into the wagon and closed the tailgate. Then she jumped out again and took Big Red's Buckskins down off the side. Now they looked like any other wagon. As soon as she was in again, she heard Big Red yelled "Haw!"

Please keep them safe Lord. I bet Tara keeps you busy in that department. Keep us all safe, please.

He rode at the side of the wagon, ready to shoot. Then the rock walls became very narrowed, and he had to ride behind the wagon. Gravel trickled down from overhead, and a shot cracked through the air and then another. Rocks splintered and splattered down on him.

"Get in the wagon!" Tara called. "You're in the way of my shots."

A bullet whizzed by his head as he dived head first into the wagon.

"Go help Big Red! I can handle the back," she yelled as she took aim and pulled the trigger.

The resulting scream had her smiling.

Zander hustled up front. There were a few holes in the canvas, and he shook his head. Their attackers had taken advantage of the wagon train's need for water, knowing they couldn't have waited the ambushers out. Thankfully, the shooters were only on one side of the canyon.

Big Red handed Zander the lines. Here, I'm a better shot. Big Red picked up both rifles and ammunition for them and jumped off the wagon. "Keep going and take a shot now and then. I'll take care of her."

Zander glanced into the back and realized Tara was gone. If he stopped, it would just alert them that Tara and Big Red weren't in the wagon. He wasn't sure what to do, so he did what he was told and kept shooting. A man fell in front of his wagon, and Zander gulped as the oxen trampled him, and then the wagon jolted right over him.

He saw Indians ahead on both sides of the canyon, and he could see the end of the canyon. Zander wanted to close his eyes. An arrow was probably aimed at him this very second.

An arrow whizzed by, but it didn't even come close to him. More arrows sailed through the air, aimed, not at him but at the men above him. A ripple of shock raced through him. The Indians were shooting at the gunmen. *Thank you, Lord, thank you.*

As soon as he was out of the canyon, he parked the wagon and started running back in. He couldn't see beyond the wagons. Where were Tara and Big Red? Finally he caught sight of them walking in front of a wagon, carrying the man that had fallen. It was a gruesome sight.

"Are you all right? Who is that man? What about the Indians?" He rattled off every question that occurred to him without giving anyone time to answer.

Tara was breathing hard. "Let me catch my breath, and I'll tell you. They walked to the canyon's edge and went to the side of the train. Tara sat and closed her eyes.

"Were you hit?" Zander looked her over but didn't see any blood.

"No, we're both fine. After the roan's rider, here, fell, there was a pause and Big Red showed himself to the Indians."

"I traded with them when I first came out here," Big Red said a bit sheepishly. "Stayed with 'em for a spell."

"This is the man who rode the roan horse in your father's attack?" Zander asked.

She nodded, no longer breathing hard.

Harrison pulled over and jumped down. After a moment, he brought them water. "That was some right fancy shooting, Big Red, Miss. Tara."

What sounded like cries of triumph came from above. Big Red stood in the middle of the trail and waved his arm back and forth. One of the Indians waved back, and suddenly they were gone.

The next wagon that stopped had Dawn inside, Zander just knew it from the crying. Having been captured, tortured and almost killed by Sioux, Dawn shook in fear whenever Indians were around.

Declan carried Luella out of the wagon and Heath had Dawn. Luella was very quiet and Dawn was beside herself.

"Big Red knows those Indians," Zander explained. "That's why they helped,"

Dawn turned her head and gazed at Big Red for a moment. "Heath, can we go sit next to Big Red for a while?"

"We sure can, sweetheart."

Captain London rode up. "We still have a ways to go until we hit that creek." Worry was etching deepening lines across his forehead.

"We'll make it, Captain," Zander said. He was confident the group could do anything it had to.

Harrison rummaged through the gunman's pockets. He found a piece of paper that looked to have been crumpled and then smoothed out many times. He looked it over and handed it to Tara. "Does this mean anything to you?"

Tara took the paper. As she read, her face paled and her hands shook. Finally, she looked up. "It's the names of the trappers on the wagon train. I don't know for sure, but the number next to my pa's name is the amount of money he carried."

"Just the trappers on your train? You recognize all the names?" Harrison asked.

"I think…" Tara glanced at the list again. "I think yes."

"Big Red, your name's not on this list… unless you go by another name?" prodded Harrison.

Big Red shook his head.

"Did you have to bring money with you?" Harrison tapped his chin thoughtfully.

"No, I had mine wired to the bank in Oregon. It's every penny I have except for my travelin' money"

Harrison took the piece of paper back. "You don't mind if I hold on to this, do you?"

Both Tara and Big Red shook their heads.

Tara stood up. "We should get going."

Dawn moved closer to Big Red. Harrison nodded at Heath as he stood.

"Why don't we have Zander drive, and Tara would you mind riding in that wagon? I don't think Dawn will part with Big Red here. Luella is good with Dawn in these situations."

CHAPTER EIGHT

 he days had become hard. The animals were getting slower and they had only found a few places to stop where there was water. They needed grass, plentiful grass, and rest as well, but the captain explained they needed to get over the Blue Mountains. People were running out of supplies. At first Tara had been generous giving to those in need only to find out some were holding supplies back in case they were really starving. To her it was the same as crying wolf, and for that, she'd never help the same people again. She'd been a good Christian and given to others, and to her dismay, she'd been taken advantage of.

She hated looking at her fellow travelers knowing they had stolen from her. At least to her it was the same as stealing. Her little group was all that mattered. She finally named her mare Hunter. Whenever Tara went out on her to look for fresh meat, they always came back with something. There had been a lively discussion about Hunter being a male name, but she didn't care, and she had held to her choice.

Finally, after another dusty and impossibly hard day, they descended along steep trails into the Grande Ronde Valley. It was a sight to behold. Grass, green lush grass was plentiful as were the trees. The water seemed to sparkle. For the first time in what seemed forever, Captain London announced they would rest a day.

For once, people weren't abuzz with excitement to have an extra day. They were too tired. Others were sick, and many of the livestock appeared half starved. There were also plenty of Indians around.

Dawn ran for the wagon as soon as it circled and jumped in. Heath was soon in there with her. It must be almost like hell for poor Dawn. Tara could only hope that wherever they settled, it wasn't near an Indian village.

The Nez Perce Indians seemed peaceful enough, and they had things to trade. People were able to get ground corn and dried meat. Tara couldn't help but wonder if the dried beef came from the dead cattle left behind by other emigrants. She traded rabbit furs for plenty of corn. If her hunting luck continued, her group would be just fine.

She also came back with a buckskin jacket for Big Red. He did more than his share of work.

He laughed when he came back from his trading trip and saw the jacket. He pulled a bead-decorated one out from behind his back for her, plus a pair of fur-lined moccasins. She laughed as she finished frying up corn cakes. She put them in a pile for the rest of her group, grabbed her fishing supplies, and headed to the river.

She stared at some of the people who had lied that they were hungry and wondered why they didn't go to the river and fish. Did they expect to have everything handed to them?

She loved the outdoors. She felt as one with nature, and for some reason that made her feel closer to God. It was a lovely thing. A few of the women were washing clothes at the creek and Tara wondered where they got their energy from. Even dainty Leona was washing out some underthings.

"What are you supposed to be doing?" Leona asked, subjecting her to a disdainful stare.

"Trying my luck at fishing. I bet there are some big fish in this river." Tara didn't have a clue what to say next, so she said nothing. It was nice and quiet for about a half hour. Tara had caught three large fish and was hoping for one more.

"You make a better man than a woman, you know," Leona told her in a scathing tone. "Most men don't like females who can do manly chores better than them. You aren't fooling anyone with those ugly dresses you wear. You still walk around like a bowlegged man. I'm surprised you haven't cut your hair short and started smoking a pipe."

Tara had to calm herself before answering. "How do you know I don't smoke a pipe?" She smiled at Leona as if she was fine.

"You don't wear a corset, do you? Then again, you have no need for one." Leona put her wet clothes into her basket and walked away.

What did that mean? A tug on her line demanded her attention, and she hauled in another fish. Now she had plenty for dinner. And now that Luella was feeling better she ate an awful lot. Cora wasn't as bad. Tara's smile faded. She'd never know what it was like to be a mother. It had been something she was trying to convince herself was fine, but it wasn't. Perhaps never was too strong a word. There might be a mate for her out there. Some day.

She gazed down the river and was startled to see a white girl in Indian garb. What on earth? The girl put her hands together as if in prayer or pleading. Was she pleading for Tara's help?

Tara gave her a quick nod and took the fish back to the wagon.

Luella teared up. "What would we do without you, Tara? You do too much for us."

Tara wiped her hands and then kissed the top of Luella's head. "I'm happy to help out. I need to talk to Dawn. Is she still in the wagon?"

"Yes, she is, and Heath could use a break."

Tara walked to the next wagon. "It's me, Tara. I need to ask Dawn's advice."

Heath put his head out of the wagon. "I'll be right out."

Tara heard them speak of their love for each other before Heath jumped down.

"Go, eat. We'll be fine for a bit."

Heath hesitated.

"I have my gun and my knife."

He smiled. "I'll be back in a little while." He helped Tara up into the wagon.

She sat down near Dawn, and Dawn hugged her. "I feel like a useless baby. I can't bring myself to even look out of the wagon."

"I don't blame you. You've been through something most wouldn't have come back from. I need your help. I was fishing, and a white girl in a doe dress caught my eye. She stared at me and held her hands like this."

Confusion flitted across Dawn's face. "Like she was praying?"

"Yes, I think she was asking for help. Can I walk up to the Chief and ask for her or about her?"

Dawn's eyes grew wide. "No. They hide all whites when others are around. What did she look like? Did she look neat and clean or was she ragged and dirty? Don't tell me all Indians are dirty."

"I know they aren't. I've broken bread with some. They were my father's friends. She looked frightened, and she didn't appear to be anyone's daughter. Her dress had holes in it, and her hair wasn't neatly braided. She wore no adornments, and there weren't any beads on her clothes."

"You're observant. We'll have to take her and hide her. Or maybe Big Red knows what to do. He's not talking to that widow woman again is he?"

"I'm afraid so. I might have to build my own home after all." Tara smiled, but it really could happen.

"Big Red will have to see what's up. If he can marry her, we can take her. If not we need a place to hide her. They'll search the wagons before we go if she's missing or they'll come after us and kill us. We need to think through all possibilities before we act."

"He's our best bet."

Abruptly, Dawn sniffed the air. "Tara, thank you for providing us with food again. I can smell the fish. How are these people going to make a life in Oregon if they don't fish? I just don't understand how they think."

"I know. All I can say is I helped and got tricked. I know not one of those I fed would think to feed me if I was without. But it really doesn't help to keep getting mad about it. It changes nothing and it ruins my mood. I thought about it the whole time I fished. Oh! Heath is here. I will tell you what's going on after talking to Big Red. What if they do a search? Will you be able to get through it?"

"As long as I have Heath I'm fine."

"You what?" Zander fairly exploded later. He shook his head as he folded his arms in front of him. "Did you get dropped on your head when you were young?"

"There is no need for insults." Then something occurred to her. "Speaking of insults; what does it mean when a woman meanly tells you that you don't need a corset?"

Zander turned crimson. "I wouldn't think it an insult. You have a tiny waist so you don't need to wear one."

"Why is it I don't think you're telling me the truth?" She huffed out her irritation. "There *is* an insult in there somewhere. I just have to figure it out. Your girlfriend told me I walk like a bowlegged man too. Don't worry, she's still in one piece. I didn't use my knife on her. This time."

He shrugged and glanced away. "When did you two have a conversation?"

"While I was fishing and she was washing her corset."

He sliced the air with one hand in a movement that reflected his impatience. "I came to find out what you are doing getting mixed up with an Indian girl."

"Can't I do anything without you finding out about it? No offense but it's starting to bother me that people report my plans to you." She pursed her lips and narrowed her eyes. "You're not asking people to report to you?"

"No, they just tell me. Especially if your plan is going to get you killed."

"There isn't a plan—yet, but we need one by the time we leave. Big Red is going over there now to make friends and see if he can find out who the girl is. We need that information to make a plan."

"If you need to hide her, where exactly do you plan to do that?" His jaw jutted out a bit, showing his anger. Too bad.

"I plan to remove the tools from the box under the wagon seat, put in a few holes for air and hide her there."

He looked surprised.

"What's wrong? Is my idea a good one?" Her lips twitched as she tried not to laugh. A stony expression was hard to perfect. "If you're done questioning me, I'm sure I have things to do."

"Such as?"

"I would bathe in the river but it's getting chilly. I think I'll heat some water and take a quick bath. Tomorrow I will wash clothes. You're welcome to bring your dirty clothes over to be washed."

"I'll haul water for your bath," he said as he picked up two buckets.

"The clothes?"

"Someone already offered, but I do appreciate you asking." His long legs made for quick strides toward the river.

How could she turn her feelings off as far as that man was concerned? She tried so hard to keep everything on a friendly level, but he always wiggled his way into her heart and then splintered it right after. She sat by the fire alone and watched the Nez Perce wander around. She patted her pocket making sure her gun was still there.

She heard a few gasps from Dawn and wished they could take her elsewhere. At least she had Heath, and he just adored Dawn. Perhaps they'd have an announcement of their own to make before the trip was through.

Zander filled the two big pots with water and put them over the fire and then he went to get more water.

Tara tried not to watch him walk away, but she wanted—she needed—to store away as many memories of him as she could. She knew now there would be no other for her.

"What are you thinking about so intently?" Big Red asked as he sat down.

Tara got up and poured him a cup of coffee then handed it to him.

"Thank you." He took a sip and then another. He was taking too long.

"I got to see the girl. I guess she's a spunky one, and they think she's more trouble than she's worth. They thought me a bit old for her and are scouting out the camp for someone else but I think we have gathered enough items to buy her."

"I have money to buy things from others if needed."

"We'll know more in the morning. They've had her for a while and adopted her, but she has not adopted them and her father fears for her. According to him she is too disobedient and will probably be brought to heel by one of the warriors."

"What about sneaking her away?"

Big red shook his head. "They will hunt us down until they have killed every one of us. I could try to adopt her. Wait. One of the men close to the chief is signaling me. I'll be back."

What if Big Red got hurt? It would be all her fault.

Lord, please don't let this end in tragedy. Big Red is a good, kind man and I love him, Lord. And Lord, I also love Zander Kennedy, but he doesn't love me back. Help me to guard my heart. Thank You for getting us this far safely. It's been a much longer and very much harder trip than I ever imagined, and I know many keep going because of their faith in You. You are our light in so many ways. You guide us, You teach us right from wrong. You expect us to act kindly to each other and You expect us to forgive. There is so much more You do. You give us hope and comfort and You listen. Your love is unconditional. The more I read the Bible the more I try to understand it. We are all sinners at some point, but if we repent, if we are truly sorrowful, You forgive us. Truthfully, I used to think that when something bad happened and people would just say it's God's will, that was something people made up because they had no other answer. Sometimes it's hard to remember that You know best and You have a plan for each of us. What I don't understand is if You set me on a path and I veer off that path, if it's part of Your plan or did I go against Your plan? I have a lot to think about Lord. I do know if I take the wrong path You are there to put me on the right one. I suppose I have to be listening to You. I'm strong willed, and I've probably twisted Your path for me many, many times. Yet You are right here with me. I don't know why my father died like he did. I can't reconcile that with being Your will. Maybe there is good and bad in this world and some-

times the bad people aren't stopped. I'll continue reading Your book. Maybe faith is not having to have all the answers. Maybe it's just believing in You.

"HERE'S MORE water for you. Would you like me to pour it into the wash tub?"

"Yes, thank you. I'll hang blankets. Do you think you could stand guard?"

"Of course."

She didn't like the concern she saw in his eyes. Everything was going to be just fine. After the bath was ready and the blankets hung, Tara felt secure that no one could see in. She undressed and picked up a cake of soap she had found in one of the trunks. It smelled like flowers.

She scrubbed herself and washed her hair. If she'd had the time she would have loved to soak for a while, but she needed to find out about Big Red. She stepped out of the tub and dried herself putting on her chemise and dress. She quickly braided her hair, so it hung down the front of her shoulder.

When she walked out from behind the blankets, the expressions on both Zander and Big Red's faces set her heart racing.

"What's wrong?"

"They want Zander here as a husband to that little gal," Big Red said sadly.

"What?"

"I lied to them, and I don't see any way to undo the lie. I told them Zander was married to you. Her father thinks I'm lying and if you and Zander don't prove you're married, it won't go well for me."

She glanced at Zander and noted how his eyes glittered. He was furious she could tell. "I could just tell them."

101

Zander shook his head slowly. "They want to see us going into the wagon together as man and wife."

Her mouth dropped open. "This has become such a mess."

"That's why people need to talk to me before they act," Captain London said from behind her.

She jumped and then turned. "You're right, I should have. She's white and she wants my help, but it's not going as I thought it would,"

"These things never do." The captain sighed.

Big Red filled the captain in, and the captain actually laughed.

Tara furrowed her brow. "What's so funny?"

"Everyone with eyes can see you and Zander are in love. Let's get Minister Paul, get you two hitched and let them Nez Perce see you go into the wagon. In the meantime, we'll get them to trade for the girl. Who will be responsible for her? How old is she?"

"She's ten," Big Red answered.

"Good Golly! They expected to marry her off?" The captain muttered a few choice words under his breath.

Zander stood, and she was afraid he'd walk away. Instead, he held his hand out to her. "We need to talk."

She nodded and walked with him toward the river.

He shifted his weight from one foot to another. "I can't in good conscience leave that girl behind. I think it best if we marry and Big Red adopts the girl. I'm assuming you and Big Red planned to live together?"

Her heart thumped hard. "I figured we would, but we never made plans."

"We could help him raise her. That's if he wants the job."

She tilted her head and stared at him. Why hadn't he objected to the marriage? "I thought Dawn would be the logical choice. They both lived with Indians."

"I don't think that would work. Heath and Dawn are

making their way, and Dawn still has nightmares. I just think it's too early in their marriage for them to raise a child they don't know."

She closed her eyes briefly and tried to make her expression normal. It wouldn't be too early in her and Zander's marriage since he probably didn't expect to stay around. They didn't need to get used to being married. She should be grateful he was willing to help but her heart began to ache.

"Let's get married now. It's almost bedtime." She led the way to their fire where Reverend Paul and his wife Della already waited.

She managed to squeeze out a smile for everyone. She said all the right words and received a kiss on the cheek from Zander, all while her heart crumbled. While waiting for Big Red to come back with witnesses, she watched Zander and Leona have a lively discussion. It wasn't a happy one, and it ended with Leona running to her wagon in tears.

Tara was at the end of her emotional rope. She climbed unassisted into the wagon and began making room for the two of them. When she heard Big Red's voice she stood at the back of the wagon and smiled as Big Red swung her down. He took her hand and led her away from the wagon.

"I'm pleased you're married to the man you love, but I see shadows and sorrow in your eyes. I should have just said no and never told you getting married would help. I only wanted happiness for you."

"Well since you'll be adopting her, I'm supposed to help raise her. I thought maybe Dawn should, but Zander thinks her marriage is too new to bring in an unknown child. I guess it shows what he thinks of our marriage." She gulped in air to keep from weeping. "I need to have faith we're doing the right thing, but Big Red it hurts something awful. I guess it will be the three of us making a life in Oregon and it'll be just fine. Zander never wanted to marry. But I think—" Her voice hitched. "I believe we'll be just fine." She lifted her arms, and he bent so she could wrap them around his neck. Then he lifted her into a hug and carried her to the wagon.

"I love you, Tara."

She nodded and went inside. It had been a long hard day made even harder and exhaustion hit her. She lay on the straw tick, still clothed, and waited.

THE NEXT MORNING, Zander watched as Tara's horse was exchanged for the young girl. He found out her name was Rhetta Knobs. Tara was still sleeping and he'd been getting sly looks all morning.

Cora and Luella helped Rhetta to bathe and dress. She was a pretty girl with long dark hair and green eyes. She'd been walking alone and was stolen and adopted. She'd been with the Nez Perce for about a year. They set her by the fire while they quickly took a dress someone had donated and cut it down then sewed it back up in her size. It was a very simple blue one, but the ladies who were helping all said they'd make more.

Rhetta seemed to be very quiet and reserved. Not the unmanageable girl Zander had been led to believe she was. She watched everything and sat close to Big Red.

"I'm going to make sure the oxen are grazing. Sometimes you have to lead them to the better grass. If Tara wakes before I'm back, can you tell her I'll see her soon?"

"Will do," Big Red said with a bit of suspicion in his eyes.

Big Red had nothing to worry about, Zander thought bitterly. His precious Tara was still untouched.

Zander felt shanghaied into the marriage, but he went along with it to keep the peace. Now he had his regrets. Not because the marriage hadn't been consummated. He just didn't know his own mind and didn't appreciate others making decisions for him. He'd gotten as far as the Blue Mountains without getting hitched.

Now what? Were he and Tara supposed to sleep in a tent while Rhetta slept in the wagon with Big Red underneath? He never should have gone to the fire last night to see what Tara was up to. He should have minded his own business. Tara was lovely, for certain, but if a man had any type of aspirations she'd pull him down. Would she go back to wearing her buckskins now that she didn't need to look nice? Oh sure, and he didn't mind them, but for presenting herself to townsfolk? No matter where they lived, people wouldn't take kindly to her wearing them. He'd probably have to teach her manners the town women would expect from a wife. Not that he was even an expert. They'd peg him for a backwoods dweller with no education. Did she know how to set a table? What about pouring tea for women who'd come calling? If Leona wore a corset, Tara probably should too. He wanted to elevate his position in life, and in America he'd hoped to do so.

Irritation washed over him at the sudden change in his plans.

They had slept back to back last night, and he was the one who stiffened if they happened to touch. She just muttered and moved. She had money, though. He patted one ox and shook his head. He supposed some men—most really— would consider what was hers to now be theirs. But not him. Her money was hers, and he shouldn't be thinking of his wife in such a way.

In truth, he couldn't complain about Tara being his wife. He'd have liked to have been the one to decide to marry or not, was all.

He was walking back toward the wagons when Leona stepped out from behind one and blocked his way.

"Why? You trifled with me and then you married another? Why?" Tears started to spill down her face, and she flung her arms around him and buried her face in his chest. He gently patted her back wishing he could just walk away. But nothing she said was false. He had shown her interest and he had married another woman.

Tara and Rhetta rounded a wagon and almost ran into them. Hurt flared in Tara's eyes, then she looked down at her feet as though shamed while Rhetta narrowed her hardened eyes.

Tara stepped away. "Sorry, I didn't know you were here." She didn't look at them. She walked to the river with Rhetta following her, each carrying a bucket.

"Leona, you need to let go of me. I'm married." Zander gently set her away. "I never trifled with you. I never kissed you."

"Still you led me to believe you were falling in love with me." A sob escaped as she turned and ran to her wagon.

He never meant for anyone to get hurt. He didn't like Leona as a person let alone a wife. It was as though he was in the middle of a bad dream and he couldn't wake up. He needed to get away from her. He'd best go make sure the wagons were in good shape.

By the time he got to the wagons they had all been taken care of. What was he supposed to do? Big Red already had the wash tub on the fire heating water. He grabbed his clothes out of the wagon he'd shared with his friends and put them in a pile next to the fire.

"Rhetta seems like a good girl," Big Red said.

"Yes she does but didn't they say she was too much to handle?"

Big Red laughed. "As soon as she is away from here, she'll show that side of her. She'll be keeping me busy."

"None of the other women have objected to you adopting a girl. I mean you don't have a wife."

Big Red shrugged. "I expected some upset, but no. They know that Tara is with me too."

"Not really, since she's my wife."

Big Red sat down poking more branches under the wash tub. "Is she? I know you haven't even been married for a whole day yet, but you've held Leona more than you have Tara."

Ire rose within his chest. "How can you possibly know that?"

"I saw Tara when she came out of the wagon this morning. Her bottom lip was trembling, and she was wearing the same thing she had on yesterday. I handed her a cup of coffee and she wouldn't meet my gaze. She didn't even react when I told her the mare had been traded. You see, my Tara is feisty. She's not a sad woman. Then I saw you with Leona and what happened when Tara met up with the two of you. You still had your girlfriend in your arms. You surely didn't act sorry, but I could tell by Tara's reaction that she'd sunk as low as she could go. She's been through an awful lot in a short amount of time, and she never took a moment to mourn or feel bad, but now…"

Zander nodded. "I have bridles to check and repair." He walked away as quickly as he could. He looked over the tack and then found a place to sit by the river where he couldn't be seen unless someone came looking for him.

It was too early to go back to the wagon. He wasn't sure what to do. Why couldn't he just jump on a horse and ride away?

"Here he is, Declan," Heath called.

Heath and Declan each sat on one side of him. "Sorry about how things happened," Declan said.

"No one said anything to us about this. We were

surprised by the marriage too. Dawn thinks you're a hero," Heath said.

"I wasn't given a choice, and she's upset. She walked by when Leona was crying and telling me she had been thinking I'd marry her. Leona also had her arms around my neck. Both Tara and Big Red are angry, but I'm angry too. I'm glad we saved the girl, but I'm tied to Tara for life. I can't picture staying home, raising kids."

"It looked to me as though you and Tara were getting close," Declan said.

"A little at a time. We're very different, and we tend to read each other wrong. I've hurt her, and she's hurt me, and it's all been misunderstandings. We decided to be friends and see what happened. Big Red said she came out of the wagon this morning ready to cry. I didn't even touch her. I haven't had an awful lot of happiness in my life and I always thought my wedding day would be a happy one. I'm frustrated about the whole situation, and somehow it's my fault. I swore when I got off that ship in Boston I would be free. And now?" He snorted a sarcastic laugh. "I don't know how to talk to her or how to act around her."

"Listen Zander," began Declan. "None of us expected to get married for a long while. I wanted to get the ranch going and a house built first, but things happen. I was forced to marry too, and I thank God every day for Luella. Look at Harrison. He was grieving his dead wife when he ended up marrying Cora. Heath here, I secretly think he got what he wished for. Nothing is easy for any of us. We all have to work with our wives to learn to love and learn how to get along. There have been so many who have died making this trip. We're at the bottom of the Blue Mountains. We make it over these mountains, then the Cascades, and then we're in the valley of land and opportunity. You have to remember Tara lost her father not too long ago." Declan patted Zander on the back.

Harrison wandered over. "Cora is putting together a picnic for you and Tara. You need some time to get to know each other. Life is too short to be miserable. I know first-hand. Plus we saved a young girl. That's a good thing. I haven't had a chance to talk to her. Are there people looking for her?"

"She has a family somewhere. We'll get it figured out." Zander stood. "I've been alone for so long, you can't imagine how I feel now, knowing I have friends who care. Thank you."

"Friends?" Heath chuckled. "Who said anything about friends? We're family."

Zander smiled and looked toward the wagons. He might as well go and see what Tara was up to. He cared for her, but he still had his doubts. Would they ever work through them? Doubts or not, she was his wife and he needed to act like a husband.

CHAPTER NINE

The Blue Mountains were enough to make anyone agitated. The first day was a long steep hard drive and although the oxen had rested, many were at the point they could no longer go on.

Tara willingly left many of her trunks behind to lighten the load. She only kept things they used every-day and warm clothes. Quilts were a must. She hadn't realized her father's things were still in the trunks.

Big Red was excellent driving the oxen, and they trusted him. The climb wore her out, and Rhetta didn't have much to say.

Tara worried about Cora and Luella. They should be riding in their condition, but that wasn't the way things happened. They walked under a thick canopy of trees, and when they got to the top, they stopped. And the trail was just flat for a few miles after that, at least.

The men had a hard time with the cattle and horses, and she worried. Zander and Heath didn't make it back for supper.

She still didn't know what to think about her and Zander.

He promised to keep his vows and he swore he had never touched Leona. She believed him. He had a slight twinkle in his eyes when he gazed at her, and that warmed her and thawed her cooling heart.

He'd held her that night but nothing more. She was too embarrassed to ask her friends if it was normal to just sleep. She did finally find out about the corset insult. Leona meant she didn't have a nice figure including bosoms a man would be interested in. She'd laughed as Luella turned red explaining it to her. "I am as God made me, so that can't be a real insult. To think I spent time wondering about it."

She set out crates and made the women sit. Dawn didn't want to, but Tara had heard about Dawn's torn up feet. Rhetta was a great help and soon they all sat, said grace, and ate.

"Tara, you have so much energy," Luella exclaimed.

"I'm used to moving, not sitting. Where I'm from, you don't work you don't eat, and sometimes the game wasn't near where I was. I'm used to walking a long ways up and down mountains. Tomorrow looks to be just as bad going down. Feel free to lean on me."

Cora beamed at her. "You know, I wasn't sure what to make of you when you joined us. You have a very generous soul."

"She sure does," Zander said as he kissed Tara on the cheek.

"Sit down. I'll get a wet cloth, I know it was branches that got to you but you look like you were dancing with a bear." She hurried and got a wet cloth, and then she cleaned each cut and scratch.

"How'd we do?" Harrison asked.

"We did fine. It's the others that lost some. Only a few of ours tried to stray. They did, however, take the path with the most trees."

"I can drive tomorrow and free up one of the men," Tara offered.

Harrison looked her over. "You think you're strong enough to hold the oxen back from running down the steep hills?"

"I've driven a filled wagon down mountains many times. It was with mules, though, and we never had a covering."

"What do you think, Big Red?" Harrison asked.

"If anyone could do it, Tara could. She might not look strong, but I'll just tell you never wrestle with her."

"We'll give it a try."

She fixed a plate for Zander and handed it to him, and he didn't look at her. Her stomach began to knot. What had she done now?

"It's all right if I drive, isn't it, Zander? Is that why you're mad?"

"I don't enjoy talking about our private business in public." He finished eating, put his plate down, and left.

"I'm sorry, Tara," Harrison said. "I should have asked what he thought instead of Big Red."

"So, that is why he's mad? Oh bother, I can do things to make him much madder."

She noticed most were trying not to laugh. "You all go rest. Rhetta and I will clean up. It'll be another long day tomorrow."

"I can help," Dawn said as she stood.

Laughing, Heath swept her up in his arms and took her into their tent. Envy went through Tara. If only...

———

"TARA? ARE YOU IN THERE?" Zander called.

"Yes," she whispered.

Zander entered the tent. It was dark, and he was waiting for his eyes to adjust. "It's a colder night."

"Yes it is. I put on a pair of your socks to keep warm."

He smiled at her and then he took off his coat and boots. He climbed under the covers and pulled her back against him.

"I'm sorry I walked off like that. I didn't mean to embarrass you. I guess I was hurt that no one thought to consult me. Not that I'm in charge of you, but shouldn't I have some input?"

"Harrison apologized about asking Big Red and not you. I know you know I'm strong. I'm not one for showing off so if I have trouble I'll let Harrison know. Big Red will drive so Declan can help you with the livestock. I'll drive ours. It's lighter than most. I do need to get my money out of the other wagon in case something happens."

He was silent for a moment.

"Zander, was I supposed to ask you if I could drive the wagon before offering? I don't really know how husbands and wives do things. I don't remember a lot about my ma and pa let me do pretty much whatever I wanted."

"No, you weren't supposed to but when it's a big decision, I would like to be included in the discussion. It's dangerous to drive down a mountain, and if going down is as steep as coming up was there could be many problems. I don't want you getting hurt."

"That's sweet."

"Tara, do you even like me as more than a friend?" He felt her stiffen in his arms.

"Of course I like you. Zander I care for you in a way I've never cared for another. I don't know if it's love or not. I know I was jealous and hurt when I saw you with Leona. I even felt envy as I watched Heath swing Dawn up into his arms and carry her to their tent. I feel like I'm out of my natural habitat, and I don't know what to do." She sighed, then added softly, "I liked it when we kissed."

"We're on the right road then. We have time before we—"

"What? Before we what?"

His face burned. "Before we have relations."

"Oh."

He could tell by the sound of her voice she had no idea what he was talking about. "Usually when a man and woman get married, they have a wedding night together."

"Night comes after day."

He wanted to groan. "You know animals mate, right?"

"Yes."

"Good." He kissed her cheek. "Good night."

"Good night."

She sounded confused. He'd have to think on how to explain it to her. Maybe the subject wouldn't come up again until the time was right. Even as the thought danced in his mind, he discounted it. No, he really didn't think so.

———

CHAINS LOCKED the wheels and kept them from rolling as they slid down the hill with the oxen pulling. It was nerve racking but so was being chased by a grizzly. Her hands and arms were fine. She did have pain across her shoulder blades, but that would likely get better with rest.

She was doing well, and Tara had no doubt she'd get the wagon to the bottom. She'd had retrieved her money from the other wagon, and now she wore two money belts. She couldn't wait to get them off. If wearing a corset was anything like wearing the belts, she was glad she didn't need one.

She heard a commotion behind her and turned the oxen closer to the trees on the right. Something hit one of her back wheels but she hung on to the jumpy oxen with all her might. A wagon flew by, veered off the trail, and fell onto rocks below. The wagon splintered apart as the oxen screamed, and she thought she heard a woman screaming too.

Talking calmly to her oxen, she got going again, but the scream she heard bothered her. Then she heard the shots telling her the oxen had been put down. She hoped the people survived, though there was only supposed to be the driver in each wagon. It was a shame, they were almost at the bottom.

As soon as she hit level ground, she took the chains off and sighed in relief. There was yet another mountain range in the distance but they weren't far from the Willamette Valley. Would she find answers there? What had her father been planning?

She circled, and soon the men were there to care for the livestock. Tara walked back to where the wagon had fallen. She had heard a woman scream; she just knew she did. She slid down the side of the mountain and studied the wagon. Then she heard it again. She looked around and the woman must have been thrown in the crash. Carefully Tara made her way. There was much blood, but she could tell it Leona.

Tears filled Tara's eyes at the sight of a human body so broken, but she managed to get to her side. Leona was still alive. Tara quickly cut Leona's petticoats into strips and wrapped her head. It appeared her shoulder was dislocated and there was a deep gash on her calf.

"Help! We need help down here!"

Captain London and Oscar made their way down calling for more men to find a way to carry Leona back up.

"Is she alive?"

"Yes, captain, she is. Her breathing and heart seem strong."

It took much effort to place her on a board, tie her onto it and keep it level as it was lifted to the trail. Tara sighed in relief as tears fell. "I was so afraid for her."

They sent a rope down and Tara grabbed it and walked up the side.

Zander hugged her. "We were supposed to pull you up."

"Why? I was perfectly able to get up out of there."

Zander pulled back, smiled at her and hugged her again. "What am I going to do with you?"

She had no answer for him.

People praised her as she walked with Zander back to the wagons. She smiled graciously at each one. Inside, she seethed. The hypocrites. They were the same people who talked about her and made fun of her buckskins.

"What's wrong?" Zander asked as he took her into his arms and stroked her back.

"The people who seem so happy to see me today are the same ones who ridiculed me. I just don't understand people. Maybe that's why my pa lived up in the mountains. Maybe he didn't understand people either."

"I'm proud of you. I'm proud of the way you drove the wagon and how you got out of the way of the careening wagon. A couple are stuck on the trail needing new wheels because of that wagon. Then you found a hurt woman and saved her."

It felt so good to be hugged by Zander. "Who was driving that wagon? Her father is over talking to the captain."

Zander pulled back to take a look. "You know how this group works. We should know shortly."

This time the others made her sit while they cooked the meal. She sure was tired. Zander was right; within less than an hour it was known that Leona had refused to walk and her father refused to let her in the wagon assuming she'd have to walk if he didn't. She had talked another driver into letting her ride in the back. She was lucky she survived. The driver had died.

The sun was setting, and it was a beautiful sight with the reds and oranges and yellows melding together.

"Are you too tired to take a walk?"

Smiling she shook her head. "I'd be honored."

They held hands as they walked to view the valley.

"Our future is just over those mountains. Can you imagine?" Zander asked.

"I don't want to talk about the future. You resent me, I know you do. I never intended to get you wrapped up in my problems. I just happened to steal away in your wagon and it's not fair to you. And I'm sorry. I don't look like a proper wife. I know I look more like a boy than a girl. I don't have curves like Leona. I kind of thought it a blessing. I didn't have my bosom in my way while I shot an arrow or a gun. I lost my sling shot, but I'm good with that too. I'm kind and I'm smart and I have a big heart. But I don't have qualities any man would like in a wife. I think after Oregon, I'll go west. There are still trappers in Canada." She turned her face to him, tears in her eyes. "Do you understand? I'm giving you your freedom."

His mouth dropped open. "I thought you liked my kisses. I thought we wanted the same thing; to build a life together. I thought we could be happy together. You would really leave me?"

"You care for me?"

He scowled. "You're my wife."

"Oh." She quickly glanced away. "It's been a long day.

"Let's go set up the tent," she suggested.

118

FOR THE NEXT WEEK, Tara studied all the wives on the train, trying to learn what made one woman a good wife and another not so good, according to their husbands and how they treated them. She'd come to the conclusion it was that special spark they had in their eyes for each other. How to get the spark was a mystery.

So far, she tried agreeing with everything he said. He mumbled something about her being a parrot. Then she tried to improve what she had *thought* were her adequate cooking skills. Zander wasn't one to try new things, and he refused to eat weeds or dandelions. Rhetta had the best time laughing at Zander's horrified face. Smiling at him didn't work and being attentive just brought more frowns.

She tried to be cheerful, but they were traveling from sunup to sundown, and she felt herself feeling cross at him more than once. When she talked to the minister, he just said she was doing all the right things. The other women helped to buoy her spirits, but eventually that didn't work either.

She was concentrating on driving through the cascades when a wheel broke. She went careening to the other side of the bench and held on as hard as she could to the lines. The oxen stopped, and she was able to climb her way up to the brake and wrap the lines around it.

This would not be an insurmountable problem. They had an extra wheel; she'd just change it. First, she unloaded the wagon, noticing no one stopped to help or even ask if she needed her husband. She put large logs under the wagon, making a bigger base and then building upward to lift the wagon enough to get the wheel off. The logs weren't going to stay in place.

Maybe if she got the wheel off quickly and could rebuild the logs up and get the new wheel on... Or maybe she'd be pinned under the wagon. Finally, after staring at the problem for a while, she decided to reinforce the logs with large branches going from the ground up the side of the logs and then wedged against the wagon floor. It was back breaking work, but she did it.

She put more grease around the axle, took the C-shaped iron wrench and wrestled the nut off. The oxen stomped and shuffled; they were growing anxious. The brake was on, but they were antsy, making the logs move slightly. There had to be a simpler way.

She pulled the wheel off and examined it. It looked as though it could be repaired, but she wasn't sure. She would haul it with her just in case. Now to get the new wheel. She had set it next to the trunks when she unloaded the wagon. She knew they were sturdy, but they were heavier than she'd realized. She thought to just slide the new wheel on, but everything had shifted underneath. She needed to crawl beneath there to fix it.

She wiggled under the wagon, vowing to wear her buckskins from now on. She lay on her belly shoring up the logs when they all suddenly began to fall. Tara rolled, but she wasn't quick enough. Her wrist was caught under one of the heavy chunks of wood.

Pain shot up her arm and then mercifully it all went numb. She forced herself to breathe slowly and blinked back tears. Crying wasn't going to help. Maybe she could lever the log off her arm. But if she did that and failed she'd crush her wrist for sure. Instead, she took one of the branches and started digging a hole under her wrist hoping to perhaps ease it out.

Her heart beat so fast she feared she would lose consciousness, so she waited for it to slow before she started. Meanwhile, wagons went rolling right by. Did they not see her feet? She sincerely hoped they hadn't. It was unthinkable that people knew and didn't offer help.

The pain was setting in again, but she gritted her teeth and kept digging. It was slow going with just a branch.

"Tara! Tara are you hurt?" Harrison yelled as he got down on his knees and looked under the wagon. "What in the world?"

"Broken wheel." That should have been explanation enough, but by the way he stared at her she had done it all wrong.

"Is anything else pinned beside your wrist?"

"No. I need a small shovel or a big spoon."

Gravel crunched beneath his feet as he strode away. She waited for him to come back. When he did, he handed her a big spoon.

"I'm going to have to look at this from all angles. Will you be fine while I look?"

"Yes." She tracked his position with her ears as he made his way around the wagon. Then she heard horses' hooves and Zander's voice. He'd think she was stupid, useless even, and that thought hurt more than her wrist.

Zander slid under the wagon next to her and took the spoon from her. He dug while watching the logs. A few were still piled. "We should have you out in a minute."

He dug hard and fast and at last she was able to wriggle her wrist out from under the log. It throbbed badly. He yelled to Harrison to pull her out. As soon as she was free, he rolled out and closed his eyes. Then he stood and looked at her with fury in his eyes.

"What do you think you were doing? You could have been killed!"

"I—"

"I don't want to hear it. Just stand over there out of the way." His tone was gruff and uncaring.

She hung her head and stood where he had pointed. Harrison grabbed a wooden tool and the next thing she knew he had the wagon lifting up. Then he put the wheel on and secured it with the nut.

Zander pulled all the logs out of the way and then the branches. He kept glancing at her and shaking his head.

Tugging at the bottom of her sleeve, she tried to hide her injury.

"I'll be driving for a bit." Zander tied his horse to the back of the wagon. He hardly looked at her and then he left. Harrison got back on his wagon and followed.

The realization struck her that there was a difference being alone and being all alone. Obviously neither of the men thought much of her. They could have at least asked how she was. It grew hard to breathe, her chest was so tight. *I will not cry, I will not cry, I will not cry.*

She hurried her walk so she wouldn't have to talk to anyone, but after a while the pain was so excruciating she stepped off the trail and found a tree to sit under. Taking her knife she cut off the hem of her dress and tightly wrapped her swelling wrist. Then she awkwardly made herself a sling after she cut yet more of her dress. At least they were almost at their destination. After the last wagon went by, she carefully stood and got back on the trail. She hoped there was water where they would stop. Cool water would help with the swelling.

Oh Pa, why aren't you here?

The pain made her sick to her stomach, and she had to stop many times, but she made it in before dark. No one had bothered to ride out to find her. All alone was a heartbreaking feeling. She'd never have known such heartache if they had never left their mountain.

Thankfully, there was water and she walked right by the wagons to it. She kicked off her shoes and walked into Barlow Creek where she took off her sling and unwrapped her wrist. The water was cold but there was no help for it.

Letting her arm drop her wrist went right into the wonderful frigid water. It felt better already. Much better.

After wrapping the sling around her neck she massaged her wrist until her feet were numb. She'd have to walk downstream for a bit to find an easy way to exit the creek. It was a farther walk than she imagined, and when she went to get her shoes, they were gone. Her fur-lined moccasins had disappeared.

They wasn't anything she could do about it so she wrapped her wrist back up with the wet cloth and put her arm in the sling. Dread filled her as she slowly walked to the wagon. She still had dinner to make. The fire already burning almost made her smile. Looking down a few wagons she saw her group of friends all eating and having a good time. She grabbed her cup and scooped some water out of the water barrel and went into her tent. She wasn't in the mood to talk to anyone. If they had cared they would have looked for her.

She had to practically tear the dress to get it off, and then she lay on the bed. It was so cold even after she piled the quilts on. Wool socks would have been great, but she wouldn't have been able to put them on. She lay there wondering what exactly her sins had been. Yes, she'd made a mistake, but she had done her best. Tears came, and this time they wouldn't be stopped.

CHAPTER TEN

*T*he next morning Zander woke to find Tara already gone. He quickly dressed. They'd had some misunderstanding last night. Della, the minister's wife told him she would pray with Tara. At first, he'd wondered how long praying could last, but he was assured by Heath and Declan she was probably having supper with them.

It wasn't until it got late that he walked to the minister's camp and found his fire banked for the night. He ran back to his own tent, and there she was sleeping. Why hadn't she come to the fire to get him?

Upon exiting the tent, he didn't see her either. The fire wasn't going, and the coffee pot was empty. Where *was* she? He walked around the circle of wagons and finally spotted her in the creek. She was downstream. Gazing at her for a moment her realized she was hurt. He ran down to where she was.

"Tara, you're hurt!"

She didn't answer him she turned her back on him instead. He took off his boots and nearly cried out at the frigid water. How could she just stand there? He cupped her shoulders and turned her. When he saw her wrist he gasped.

"This happened yesterday?"

"Why do you think I couldn't drive? But you never asked how I was. Neither did Harrison, for that matter, and he saw my wrist pinned under a heavy tree trunk too." She shook her head. "I'm getting too soft hearted. I've started to rely on you and my friends, but I was better off alone. I'm so stupid thinking any of you would see my pain or try to help me. Didn't you even care where I was? It was so cold last night that I swear I shook most of the night. If being married means my feelings get hurt at every turn, then it's not for me. I tried to be what you wanted–wearing dresses, making extra special food, agreeing with you. But it got me nowhere. I'm just me, and I will not apologize for it. Now as soon as I find out who stole my moccasins, I'll be on my way."

Irritation sparked into anger, and he snapped, "No, you will not be on your way!"

"Why, Zander? You're not done ignoring me? Not done making me feel like I don't belong? I tried it your way, and I'm not up for any further abuse. You don't even like me." She trudged through the water and walked onto the bank. Then she wrapped her wrist again and put the sling in place. "Don't get Big Red involved in this. He has someone who needs him."

She stalked off bare footed.

He jumped out of the freezing water and followed his wife. She was absolutely infuriating! He stopped. Her wrist was all colors of purple and it looked double the size of her wrist and what did she mean someone took her shoes?

He scanned the camp and saw her moccasins on some-one's feet. He rounded their wagon and gritted his teeth. "Leona those moccasins don't belong to you."

"I know, but Eli gave them to me. He said they would help

me heal. I want to heal, you know," she replied crossly.

"Tara was the one who found you and she climbed down a cliff to see if you were still alive. Just give me the moccasins." He held out his hand trying to think of other things than wringing Leona's neck.

"Tara told me to keep them."

"When was that?"

"A minute ago. She claimed they were hers, and I told her she was mistaken and she needed to leave a fine Christian woman like myself alone." Leona smiled. "I'm keeping them."

"You will not," her father growled from the front of the wagon. "You've caused enough trouble this trip. You will return those moccasins to their rightful owner."

Leona pouted the whole time she took them off and flung them at Zander. He didn't care how he got them, the main thing was he had them.

He went to the wagon and found Big Red making breakfast with Rhetta's help. Zander could have used a cup of coffee, but he needed Tara more. Without a word, Big Red motioned toward the tent with his head. Zander nodded his thanks.

He walked right into Tara as she was trying to leave the tent. She was carrying a burlap bag.

"At least put on your boots before you go." He walked further into the tent and set the boots on the middle of the tick mattress covered with quilts. "I see you've packed up. Take a pair of my socks. I know you get cold without them. How are you going to feed yourself with a hurt wing?"

She glanced at him and then sat on the bed. She reached for her boots and started putting them on.

"Tara, I have been the worst husband. I'm so sorry. You've never seen a wagon jack before, have you?"

"I didn't know to look for one. I thought my way was sound until things began to shift. Why didn't you or

Harrison ask me if I was all right? It had taken everything I had not to scream with the tree trunk pinning my wrist."

"Honey, there was hardly enough room for wagons to get around you, and you were at the top of a hill. A couple more feet and there was a steep decline. I should have put you in the wagon, and Harrison figured I took care of you. I'm sorry." He drew a deep breath and swallowed past the lump of emotion in his throat. "Then Della said she was going to pray with you for healing when you got into camp. She can be long winded at times, and by the time I went to see what was keeping you, their fire had been banked. I came to the tent, and you were shivering so I got into bed and held you close to warm you up. I have to admit the contented sighs you made while you were in my arms warmed my heart."

He kneeled in front of her and gently put her moccasins on for her. "Please don't leave me. Please, Tara, stay and be you, just you. I don't want a woman who wears a dress when she'd rather wear buckskins. Plain cooking is the best cooking. You're already a great cook, so don't change things to impress me. If you'd rather skin a rabbit than make dresses, that's fine too. I… well, it's hard to say. I've never really said this to anyone… well maybe my ma with I was a lad. Tara, I love you with my whole heart, and I need you to be gentle with it. The fear of having another person leave me has kept me from committing to you wholly." He searched her eyes for any sign that she returned his feelings.

She swallowed hard and kneeled in front of him. Using her uninjured hand she stroked the side of his face. "Your heart will always be safe with me. I—"

Zander pulled her into his arms and kissed her deeply. She was his, really his, and they'd have a good future. Of that he was certain. He hadn't counted on Tara coming into his life, but he knew she was in it to stay.

"Thank You Lord. Thank You, thank You, thank You."

*T*ara sat by the big fire in the middle of their wagon circle. They decided for now to just live out of the wagons in a central area. They had so much land and plans and ideas kept coming. Harrison got his cattle settled and they built a corral for the horses not far from the wagons.

She had gotten an extra surprise when they first arrived in town. The sheriff asked if any of them was Patrick Carmichael. Tara and Zander met with the sheriff. It seemed that Tara's dad had bought a lot of land. All filled with trees.

"Come let me show you your saw mill."

Tara and Zander exchanged shocked expressions.

"It's on the outskirts of town and it's the biggest building in the area. It employs many from town and has been a Godsend. Well for most anyway. This mill has been sold to many by swindlers. A group of men have talked whole wagon trains to give them all their money. They tell them they are riding ahead to get things started but when the folks arrive, they find your father's mill. I'm sorry your father never got to see it. Drew the plans himself and it's called Carmichael and friends.

"From the correspondence I received, your father knew many of the men coming to start new lives didn't know a lick about farming or ranching and they'd need jobs. With so many coming to live, they'd need wood for houses and furniture. He was very smart and I was looking forward to shaking his hand.

"A man named Hogan Best runs the mill. Another man Sam Mason runs the furniture store. Your father had it named Tara Furniture. I know he relied on his trapper friends to help cut the trees but truthfully I think you'll have enough men. We'll need the names of the other men in case there are heirs."

"Yes, there is a list of how much each man had with him. How'd he get it up and running if the money was with the trappers?"

"He'd opened a bank account here a while back and ended up putting a lot of money into it. He took out a small loan which you might want to see when the first payment is due. The mill had been getting steady business."

"Take a look around. I have a meeting with someone named Big Red about a gal you all found." He tipped his hat and was gone.

"I know both the men my father hired and they are fine, honest and hardworking. I guess the scam was making so much money my father was killed so they could keep it going."

Zander squeezed her hand. "Don't forget somehow it was known they were carrying money."

"I don't mean to sound bitter but it amazes me what

people will do for money. Let's go see if Rhetta's family is here to get her."

They walked in the road hand in hand smiling. Tara finally found out what a wedding night was and she loved the closeness she now had with Zander.

"I think we still must be careful. We don't know if Crane and Bennet are still alive. We should give the sheriff a description of the men," Zander said.

"Yes, we should. Oh no, something must be wrong. Rhetta is crying." The hurried over and Tara took Rhetta into her arms.

"What happened?" Zander asked Big Red.

Big Red sighed. "Rhetta's family is not of mind to come and get her or send money for her return. I'd gladly pay for it but it seems to me they don't want her. They never told the authorities she was missing."

"Rhetta I know it's hurtful but I think you'll find that your new family loves you and would do anything to find you," Zander said.

Dawn came closer. "I feel like we are sisters. I know all of us consider the others family. All you have to do is figure out how big you want your room to be."

Rhetta eased out of Tara's arms and hugged Dawn.

"Touching, ain't it Eddie?" Chuck Klass laughed loudly. "And all that love will get you through the winter."

"Dead before the new year. That's what I'm betting on," Eddie said.

"Oh, so what is your plan? It's already September." Tara took a step.

"Chuck and I bought us shares of a saw mill. We're going to be rich."

Tara could barely keep her lips from twitching. "Sounds like you're all set. Good luck to you." She turned away.

THEY MADE their own little train going to the land they filed for. They obtained good land next to the land Tara's father purchased. Their holdings were so vast they decided to make camp at the first good sight with water.

They circled their wagon but were much farther apart than before. A big fire was made in the center and the women all helped to cook. Tara was on her way to get more water.

"Of course you can call me Pa. I'd me so proud if you did. You are one of the best jewels on earth and I'm glad you're mine. I'll do my best to protect you and teach you. I already love you."

Rhetta sobbed and went to Big Red putting her arms as far as they would go around his waist. He kissed the top of her head and his eyes were moist.

Tara smiled and mouthed I love you, before she continued on to the stream. "Pa you would have loved it here. Open land and I bet there's good hunting. I made it and don't you worry; I'll keep an eye on your saw mill."

"Where have you been? You missed the announcement." Zander smiled.

"I've been gone for a minute. What could I have missed?"

"Dawn made a run for the bushes.. And I heard it's not the first time."

Tara's mouth formed an O. "We'll have our turn next. I just know it."

"Let's get through this winter. Right now we're trying to figure out if we should quickly build one big house or two smaller ones."

"Do I get a say in any of this?"

"Of course you do."

"Two houses that we can turn into bunkhouses when we

each build our own house in the spring. How about a dogtrot in between the houses?"

"Tara that's not a bad idea. Who sleeps in what house?"

She laughed. "Why, the women in one and the men in another."

He pulled her close. "Then how are we going to have that baby?"

She put her arms around his neck and held him. "With Cora, Luella and Dawn all expecting we don't need to be in such a hurry," she whispered in his ear.

"I'm sure we'll figure that all out. As long as I'm with you I don't care. We have a lot to do before winter and time isn't on our side."

Tara took a step back. "I know. We have wood and I have to admit I'm good with a hammer. I can find berries and any other wild edible plant like onions or carrots and can them. Plus we have enough money to buy what we need. Oh and don't forget, the hunting here must be great! I can't wait! We'll need plenty of firewood. Wonder if we can get that from the sawmill too? You know before they saw it all up?" She took his hand. "Then we can spend all winter figuring how we want things. I can make a big map—"

"Tara Kennedy you are a whirlwind of wonder. I was blessed the day you snuck into that wagon. You make me proud to be your husband."

"You are so sweet. I can make you a pair of buckskins. You'll be happy when winter comes to have them."

"Look over there, Tara. The sun is setting and I think we should relax and enjoy it with the others. You have great ideas but others will have some too."

She smiled and kissed his cheek. "This learning how to interact with others isn't easy. We'll see how it all turns out. I love you."

"I love you too."

. . .

THANK you all for reading this series. Next will be The Christmas book that will go to this series nine years into the future. It has been one of the busiest years of my life and not just writing. My 18 month old granddaughter Mavis has been living here with my son for almost a year. She's a joy but I had nice schedule which you all know is now her schedule. I squeeze in my writing when I can. I do know all the words to the Wiggles songs- she loves that show.

It looks like rapid release of books is how to stay visible on Amazon So I'll get them out as quickly as possible. There 5 million books on Amazon. Hard to imagine. Thank you so much for reading my books

Kathleen Ball

ABOUT THE AUTHOR

Sexy Cowboys and the Women Who Love Them...
Finalist in the 2012 and 2015 RONE Awards.
Top Pick, Five Star Series from the Romance Review.
Kathleen Ball writes contemporary and historical western romance with great emotion and
memorable characters. Her books are award winners and have appeared on best sellers lists including: Amazon's Best Seller's List, All Romance Ebooks, Bookstrand, Desert Breeze Publishing and Secret Cravings Publishing Best Sellers list. She is the recipient of eight Editor's Choice Awards, and The Readers' Choice Award for Ryelee's Cowboy.
Winner of the Lear diamond award Best Historical Novel-
Cinders' Bride
There's something about a cowboy

facebook.com/kathleenballwesternromance
twitter.com/kballauthor
instagram.com/author_kathleenball

OTHER BOOKS BY KATHLEEN

Lasso Spring Series

Callie's Heart

Lone Star Joy

Stetson's Storm

Dawson Ranch Series

Texas Haven

Ryelee's Cowboy

Cowboy Season Series

Summer's Desire

Autumn's Hope

Winter's Embrace

Spring's Delight

Mail Order Brides of Texas

Cinder's Bride

Keegan's Bride

Shane's Bride

Tramp's Bride

Poor Boy's Christmas

Oregon Trail Dreamin'

We've Only Just Begun

A Lifetime to Share

A Love Worth Searching For

So Many Roads to Choose

The Settlers

Greg

Juan

Scarlett

Mail Order Brides of Spring Water

Tattered Hearts

Shattered Trust

Glory's Groom

Battered Soul

Romance on the Oregon Trail

Cora's Courage

Luella's Longing

Dawn's Destiny

Terra's Trial

Candle Glow and Mistletoe

The Kabvanagh Brothers

Teagan: Cowboy Strong

Quinn: Cowboy Risk

Brogan: Cowboy Pride

Sullivan: Cowboy Protector

Donnell: Cowboy Scrutiny

Murphy: Cowboy Deceived

Fitzpatrick: Cowboy Reluctant

Angus: Cowboy Bewildered

Rafferty: Cowboy Trail Boss

Shea: Cowboy Chance

The Greatest Gift

Love So Deep

Luke's Fate

Whispered Love

Love Before Midnight

I'm Forever Yours

Finn's Fortune

Glory's Groom

Made in United States
North Haven, CT
28 May 2024

53037996R00093